Anna felt her

'I think you've n[...]
crystal-clear. You don[...] not "after you" in any sense!'

'Hoity-toity, Sister Chancellor!' Daniel folded his arms, and grinned. 'And may I say in turn that you have made *that* point clear before. There's no need to rub it in. I know a high fence when I see one!'

Janet Ferguson was born at Newmarket, Suffolk, and during her going-out-to-work days was a medical secretary working in hospitals both in London and the provinces. It was when she moved to Saltdean in Sussex that she settled down to writing general fiction novels, then moved on to medical romance. She says, 'As to where I get my ideas for plots—writers are *always* asked that—they come when I'm walking my dog on the Downs. The wind whispers them into my ear...do this..do that...say this...say that...go home and write it *now*. With the elements to inspire me, not to mention two nurses in my family, I aim to keep writing medical romance, and to "plot till I drop".'

FALLING FOR
A STRANGER

BY
JANET FERGUSON

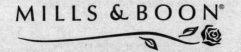
MILLS & BOON®

First published in Great Britain 2000
Harlequin Mills & Boon Limited,
Eton House, 18-24 Paradise Road, Richmond, Surrey TW9 1SR

© Janet Ferguson 2000

ISBN 0 263 82241 9

Set in Times Roman 10½ on 12 pt.
03-0006-51377

Printed and bound in Spain
by Litografia Rosés, S.A., Barcelona

CHAPTER ONE

'ANYONE would think I was going to my execution,' Anna muttered under her breath as she cycled through Trinity Lane to the hospital in Princes Parade. It was seven-thirty on a bright May morning—the kind of day to raise the spirits, make one glad to be alive.

She was returning to her post on Docherty Ward, which was Women's Orthopaedic, and it seemed as though she'd been away for years instead of only three weeks. During those three weeks she was supposed to have been married. The staff on the ortho wing had given her a rousing send-off, with a good deal of good-natured chaff—'When you return to the fold you'll be Sister *Dudley*, an old married woman!'

But it hadn't been like that, had it? She was still Sister Chancellor. Two days before the wedding had been due to take place her fiancé, Robert Dudley, had come to see her, distressed but resolute. 'I'm so sorry, Anna, I'm so very sorry, but a few days ago I met an old girlfriend again, quite by accident. The thing is, I'm still in love with her and she with me. She used to be married but now she's free, and we want to be together. I really am sorry…believe me, I'm sorry!' he repeated helplessly, looking over the sea of wedding gifts that Mrs Chancellor had set out with pride, and artistry, *and* triumph only that morning.

Anna's parents—Lois and Edward Chancellor—owned and ran the River Lawns Hotel near Silver Street bridge. Seftonbridge, with its dreaming spires and its golden, calm atmosphere, attracted tourists from all over the world, and the hotel was always full. Dons, and undergraduates, too, enjoyed the excellence of its restaurant which looked out onto the river as it wound its way to Byron's Pool.

It was from the hotel that Anna was to have been married, she and her father riding in a beribboned limousine to the church in St Mary's Square.

During the past two weeks, which should have been her honeymoon, she had nursed at a private hospital on the other side of the town, securing the post through an agency, who had gratefully snapped her up.

And would that I was still there, she thought as she began to join the stream of staff flowing in at the hospital's south gate. She could see no one she knew as yet, for the hospital was vast—seven hundred beds— which meant there were staff she never met. Palfrey Wing, the ortho wing, was Anna's domain. She knew everyone there, from high rank to low.

What were they going to say? What would they find to say to her, and what would she say in return? Her friends knew the truth, of course, as, having been invited to the wedding that never was, they had had to be informed. Anna hadn't pretended with them either when she'd rung to put them off—'Rob has met an old flame, and we've gone our separate ways.'

'It'll be yesterday's news in no time at all,' her flatmate, Julie, had said. Julie worked in the office of St Saviour's College, a very prestigious post but also a very out-of-this-world one. Julie had no idea, for instance, what hotbeds of gossip hospitals were, and ward sisters, like officers in the field, were first in the line of fire.

Anna could feel the sun warm on her back as she

bent to padlock her bike. She wore no coat, just a car-
digan over her navy sister's dress. Her long hair, the
colour of corn-on-the-cob, lay loosely coiled in her
neck. She was of medium height, slender yet curvy,
and had to watch her weight. 'You just need to cut
down on sweet things,' Rob had been wont to advise.
She'd known he'd been right, but thinking of that now
caused such a charge of fury inside her that she fairly
shot out of the sheds into the hard brilliance of the
yard, her tote bag bumping her hip.

She decided to make for the entrance to A and E,
which was the quickest way to the lifts, Palfrey Wing
being on level three of the tower block. She was halfway across the doctors' car park when she was hailed
by Daniel Mackay, Senior Registrar to Sir Guy
Morland, their orthopaedic consultant.

'Anna, wait!' He was leaning back, slamming the
door of his car—a tall, striking, black-haired Scot with
an air of authority. So he was to be her first hurdle,
was he? Anna braced herself. She was glad it was him
and no other, though, for at least he came within the
category of colleague-friend, and he wouldn't say anything trite. His opening words, therefore, were a terrible
shock. They rang in her ears like a blow. 'Good morning to you, Sister *Dudley*, and how's married life?'

This was said with a smile—more than that, with a
grin—and Anna felt sick. He couldn't have heard…he
couldn't have heard…and now she had to tell him, now
she'd have to explain. But how was it he hadn't heard?
Surely someone would have told him? And then she
remembered. Of course, of *course*, he had been away
on leave. He'd gone off two days before her, to
Scotland to see his folks. Oh, how could she possibly
have forgotten that? He had talked to her about it, had

explained why he wouldn't be able to attend her send-off party. Well, she *had* forgotten, and that was that, and now she had to explain. Her stomach rumbled audibly.

'No need to be bashful.' He laughed.

'Oh, dear.' She forced her mouth to smile, her lips sticking to her teeth. 'Evidently,' she began, 'the news of the month hasn't reached you yet. Rob and I didn't get married. We've parted for good.' And I'm not, she thought, going to say more than that. He can work it out for himself.

'Not…married!' He looked astounded, even slightly shocked.

'Riveting, isn't it?' Her gaze held his, and in his slate grey eyes she glimpsed baffled incredulity, and something else she couldn't define.

'I had no idea.' His words fell softly. 'I've not been in touch with anyone here since I went on leave. I didn't get back to my flat till midnight… I had no idea!'

'That's what I thought. I mean, you'd never have said what you did if you'd known the truth.' As she said this she realised, too late, that she'd given the game away. Now he'd know she'd been jilted, and unceremoniously.

'What can I say? The last thing I thought…' He moved her to one side as a porter, pushing a line of bedsteads, went trundling by.

'No need to say anything. Best that way.' Anna found it easier now to smile.

'You're looking good.' They began to walk on.

'I feel it. I'm raring to go.'

'Is this your first day back?' he asked, as they neared A and E's doors.

'It is, yes, but I didn't take the last two weeks as leave. I nursed at The Avenue Clinic in Downing Road…applied through the agency.'

'Sounds like a practical thing to do.' He forbore to add 'in the circumstances'.

'I enjoyed it, as a matter of fact. It gave me a new slant on nursing, and I met a lot of fresh people.' There was a crack in her voice that he didn't miss.

'Anna,' he began, then stopped as he saw Sir Guy Morland coming through from the accident ward. He was making beckoning movements and pointing to the entrance to the labs. 'Looks like I'm wanted.' Daniel touched Anna's arm and left her side, swinging his long body past the reception desk and the rows of plastic chairs.

Anna felt vulnerable, unprotected, without him, which, she told herself, was daft. She watched him join Sir Guy, saw the two of them make off down the corridor. From the back and from a distance they resembled one another, both tall and dark, Sir Guy not quite so free-striding as Daniel and very slightly stooped. He was a wonderful surgeon and a very nice man. His wife was very pleasant also. Anna had met her when she and Sir Guy had dined at her parents' hotel.

I'm amongst friends, she thought, suddenly aware of a surge of confidence. I have nothing to worry about, nothing at all. I'm here to do a job, and one that I know I do well. So, forget all about the gossip and faff, for it *will* soon blow over. Just go for it, Sister Chancellor. Take the lift up to your ward.

Up she went, across the landing and down the corridor to her office, where she found Sybil Barling, the Night Staff Nurse, writing up the report. 'Oh, Anna, hi!' Sybil pushed back her chair.

'Hi, Sybil. So, what gives?'

Embarrassment flicked between them then died. Sybil Barling gushed, 'Great to see you back. I've missed you, we all have—the patients as well!'

'Oh, I've still got some patients, then. They've not taken off in my absence?'

'*No* chance, and they keep on coming. We've got four new ones, not to mention one down in Recovery as we speak. Want to go through this?' She indicated the report, and Anna nodded, for at this time of day the night staff were thinking of home and bed.

She and Sybil sat down together, taking the entries one by one. The amputee, Margaret Patton, had been restless since three a.m., Rhoda Ventnor was off pelvic traction, but still couldn't walk without pain, young Angela Drew with a fractured pelvis had been having asthmatic attacks. The list went on, and on, and on, while across the corridor in the ward kitchen breakfasts were being prepared. Next there was a scuffle of activity as the day staff arrived—nurses greeting one another, the sound of a smothered laugh, a door slamming, a bowl crashing… Anna knew she was back.

The first thing she did, once Sybil and her underling had gone, was to look at the duty roster to see how many nurses she had—shockingly few as usual and there were two learners, she saw. Calling them in once breakfasts had been served and cleared away, she set them on their various tasks, accepting their glad-to-see-you-back comments with thanks and a smile. If there was an element of curiosity in their manner she chose to ignore it as she gave out details of the report and welcomed the two learners.

Docherty Ward had twenty-eight beds, roughly a third of which were given over to trauma cases and the rest to elective surgery—hip and knee replacements, bone-grafting and the correction of bony deformities. Athelstone—the men's ward just across the landing—was managed by Sister Fiske who was soon to retire. Big and bouncy, good-natured and cheerful, she had been very helpful to Anna, who at twenty-eight years old had been Ward Sister for only three months.

After dealing with the pile of paperwork on her desk, interviewing the senior pharmacist and placating the laundry manager who had a grouse about coloured bags, she made her round of the ward, taking one of the learners with her. As they went slowly along from bed to bed they distributed the patients' mail. Letters were looked forward to almost as much as visits, for the day could seem long when immobilised in traction, or in plaster, or both. Letters gave patients a boost and encouragement to get well fast.

One of the new patients was due for a hip replacement at nine-thirty, and would shortly have her premed. Meanwhile she was nervous and wanting to talk, and all but grabbed Anna's hand. 'I'm so afraid of the anaesthetic, Sister. What if it doesn't take? Supposing I wake up in the middle of it all and hear them sawing my bone?'

'Mrs Davis, that won't happen,' Anna reassured her. 'You'll be anaesthetised in a little room outside the theatre. When you're wheeled into the theatre, already asleep, the anaesthetist and his assistant go with you, and you're kept asleep by careful monitoring during the whole of the operation. There's no question of you waking up before everything's done. When you *do* wake up you'll be in the recovery room, where you'll be looked after for a little while, before coming back here.'

Mrs Davis looked thoughtful, but not quite so nervous. 'I wish it was this time tomorrow, with everything over and done.'

'Well, it very soon will be.' Anna smiled as her staff nurse, Jane Scott, appeared with the premed tray.

The next patient needing a sympathetic ear was Rhoda Ventnor, who had lumbar disc trouble. She had been admitted shortly before Anna had gone on leave, and had been put on pelvic traction to relieve pressure on the nerve. The treatment hadn't worked. She still had pain, even when wearing her corset, and her left foot, when she tried to walk, didn't clear the ground. She was sitting in a chair beside her bed, wearing a dressing-gown of pale green that did very little for her sallow complexion.

'I'll never be better,' she told Anna tragically. 'I put up with all that awful traction, all those weights hanging down, and I'm just as bad as when I came in here. I expect I'm incurable.'

'We don't give up on our patients, Mrs Ventnor,' Anna said firmly. 'One of the surgeons will be coming up to see you later today.'

'Looks like he's just come.' Rhonda Ventnor peered around Anna's seated form. 'It's the young one who saw me first, three weeks ago.'

Turning, Anna was surprised to see Daniel approaching, white coat untidy and undone, flying behind like a sail. She stood up and waited. Why was he here?

'Relax, Sister.' It was always 'Sister' and 'Mr Mackay' on the ward. 'I just want a word with Mrs Ventnor.' He took the chair Anna had vacated, and sat down facing the patient, asking her how she felt. After she'd told him, in detail, he asked her to walk a few steps. She did so, her strained expression and the shift of her foot on the floor confirming what the notes and she had told him.

'All right, well done,' he said, watching Anna help her back to her chair. 'I think we're going to have to get you X-rayed again, Mrs Ventnor. This time it will be a more complicated X-ray which will take more time but should show us more accurately exactly where the trouble lies. As soon as we know that, we can do something about it.' He didn't say 'operate', which Anna knew was on the cards, and perhaps Mrs Ventnor did, too.

'I'll do anything to get rid of the pain,' she said, 'and to get home again.'

'That's the spirit,' Daniel wound himself upwards and smiled down at her. 'Better ring X-Ray straight away,' he said to Anna at the ward desk. 'A full radiculogram, as you know, takes a good two hours. See how they're fixed, but press for this morning. She can have lunch when she gets back, then keep her sitting until teatime. The last thing she needs is meningeal complications with the dye.'

Leaving her to phone, he crossed the ward to speak to the scoliosis patient, Mrs Barnes, on whom he had operated six weeks ago to correct the curvature of her spine which had become so marked that it had begun to interfere with the function of the spinal cord. She was lying in a plaster bed, like a perfectly fitting shell, which was moulded to her back and hips, including the calves of her legs. Her arms were free, her head supported by a pillow on a wooden block, the complete shell being mounted on a stand with slats, roughly the height of a bed.

After six weeks Joan Barnes had adapted well to her bizarre position, passing the time by reading or listening to her radio, occasionally trying to knit. Feeding wasn't easy in the supine position, but she managed after a fashion, taking her liquids through a straw and using her special table. Toileting was embarrassing for her as she could do little for herself, except clean her teeth. 'Thank heavens,' she'd say, 'for small mercies and the use of my arms. I can still lash out if someone does something to me that I don't like!'

She was pleased to see Daniel back and told him so. At forty-eight years old she could still flirt and flatter, even from her shell.

'She's concerned about her teenage son and daughter,' Daniel said, coming back to join Anna. 'She's afraid they'll wreck the home in her absence with a lot of wild parties. As she's likely to be with us for another two months, let's hope she's wrong.'

'I've seen them when they visit.' Anna pulled a wry face. 'They're twins, seventeen years old. They're not particularly quiet in here, but Mrs Barnes shuts them up. I had to tell one of them off for smoking—*not* an easy pair.'

'How did you get on with X-Ray?' Daniel took a flying glance at the clock.

'Mrs Ventnor can go down at eleven.'

'Well done! As for me, I must take myself off.' He did so, moving with his swinging but effortless walk towards the doors.

He was due in Theatre, Anna knew. He would just about make it and get scrubbed before Mrs Davis was wheeled out of the ward.

The learner was asking what a radiculogram was, and Anna, although rushed for time, took the trouble to explain, glad that the girl had asked. 'It's an X-ray procedure taken when an ordinary film isn't precise enough. A special dye is injected by lumbar puncture, then the patient is tilted about while several pictures are taken. The dye shows up any obstruction or lesion or, as we suspect in Mrs Ventnor's case, a prolapsed disc.'

'Thank you, Sister.' The girl smiled.

'Never be afraid to ask,' Anna said with her eye on the doors as the porters wheeled in the patient from Recovery who'd been in a road accident. Her leg, with the metal fixator attached, was resting on a pillow. She was still drowsy because of painkilling drugs, but she managed to smile as Anna bent over her. She was nineteen years old with bright red, closely cropped hair and freckles across her nose.

'She's lucky to still have her leg,' Clive Stone, the senior houseman, said as he followed the porters in. 'You should have seen it when she was admitted—like something off a butcher's slab. I was amazed when Sir Guy went ahead to save it. Took us half the night, digging about for bone fragments, fitting them together with pins. I just hope she's grateful, although even now she's not out of the wood, the danger being infection, of course, or fat embolism. Still, I'm preaching to the converted, aren't I?'

His pale blue eyes made a quick top-to-toe-and-back-again survey of Anna's curvy shape. 'Just as well you're back, Sister. Good as new, I see!'

'Believe it or not, I'm glad to be back,' she told him crisply. Clive wasn't one of her favourite people. She respected him for his work, but felt he rated himself too highly for an SHO.

The morning wore on with its comings and goings. Helen the physio came first to give four patients breathing exercises and to get Mrs Hilton, one of the hip-replacement patients, out of bed for the first time. The phlebotomist, affectionately known as Dracula, came in to take blood for grouping, and the medical social worker wanted a chat with Mrs Barnes in her shell.

Very soon it was time for ward lunches, which Anna supervised, taking with her the second, more confident learner, who handed out the trays. Mrs Ventnor, back from X-Ray, and wearied from all the effort, declared that eating was beyond her, and that all she wanted was to lie down. Anna, fetching her a cup of Complan, helped her into bed but propped her up with the bedrest and pillows, cautioning her to stay that way.

'We have to keep you upright, Rhoda, till the dye in your spine passes out of your body. Later this afternoon, when the doctors are round, they'll have your X-ray result and will be able to discuss it with you and your husband when he comes. You haven't got a headache, have you?' she asked, as Mrs V. touched her head.

'It's my back that hurts, not my head,' she answered fretfully, sipping the drink Anna had brought, her eyes lowered over the cup.

Up in the cafeteria, half an hour later, Anna collected her own lunch—a tuna salad with a jacket potato—and joined Sister Fiske at her table. Apart from the senior doctors, who still had their own dining-room, all grades of staff ate together in the vast, noisy room, although even massed together there were sections of a kind— one of them being the sisters' corner, with its trelliswork of plants.

Pam Fiske was eating steak and kidney pudding with peas and creamed potatoes. 'I've been trying to get into Docherty to see you all morning,' she declared, passing

Anna the salt and giving her arm a pat. 'I'm so sorry about what happened, dear.' She took off her glasses which had steamed up, partly from the pudding but mostly from embarrassment.

'Thanks, Pam.' Anna dug into her spud.

'I didn't know whether to mention it or not.'

'I'm glad you have. If you hadn't I'd have known you were trying to!' They looked at each other and laughed.

'You're liked here, well thought of,' Sister Fiske said solemnly, following this up with, 'And you'll find someone else—in the fullness of time, that is.'

'Yes, Sister.'

'No, I'm serious, Anna, for that's the way nature works, and you could do far worse, you know, than pick someone from here. There's nothing like a shared work interest…it makes a good start. I married my Bill when he was a houseman back in our London Bridge days, thirty-five years next week, and we still get along all right—common interests, you see, as well as good sex.'

'I'm steering clear of sexual entanglements for the present. I'm starting on a period of abstinence!' Again Anna managed to laugh.

'You'll have a job with a posse of randy young doctors queuing up for a chance! Now, I bet…' Pam looked all-knowing as she pushed her plate aside. 'I bet our raven-haired, gorgeous Daniel Mackay isn't sorry Robert Dudley pulled out.'

'He said he was sorry.'

'Oh, well, them's just words!' Pam got up. 'Now, what are you having for afters, my lovely? How about some apple tart?'

'No, just coffee.'

'I'll fetch it.' She bustled off, leaving Anna to draw breath, lean back in her chair and look round the room. It was with a feeling of relief that she saw Sister Avison, from ENT, making for their table. Good, now there would be no more observations from Pam.

Dawn Avison liked nothing better than to talk about her ward non-stop. 'I cannot think *how* we're expected to carry on with such a *dearth* of nurses!' she was complaining in her strident voice as she banged down her tray.

It was just on three-thirty when Daniel and Clive Stone came onto the ward. Anna was with Kate Denver, the patient who had smashed her leg. She was far less sleepy now and wanting to talk.

'Kate was just asking why her leg couldn't have been put in plaster,' Anna said, watching Daniel glancing at Kate's charts.

'Good question.' He smiled and introduced himself to Kate, then sat down, facing her. 'A plaster in this case wouldn't have been the best idea. As well as smashed bones, you suffered extensive tissue damage, which you can see for yourself...all those fancy stitches.'

'I'm trying my hardest *not* to see.' She looked at him instead.

'All this metal cage-work, which we call a fixator,' he went on quietly, 'supports the pins and screws which are keeping your bones in place. I promise you, you'll get used to it in time, not feel so wary of it.'

'How *much* time? How long am I going to have to have it on?' She was sweating slightly, Anna noticed. She needed to rest, but as she was intent on asking questions that had to be addressed.

'Around six weeks.' The answer was gentle.

'Six *weeks*!' Her blue eyes went round.

'After that you'll have a brace fitted—a kind of plaster with a knee hinge. You'll be able to walk then with the aid of crutches, and soon after that you can go home.'

'All this because I swerved to avoid a cat and ended up wrapped round a bollard. The cat would probably have survived anyway, but I just couldn't have borne to have run over it!' she choked, and then burst into tears.

'You'll be all right.' Daniel reached for a box of tissues on her locker and pulled a handful out. While she mopped up he told her that time would pass quickly, 'much faster than you think. You'll be having physio twice a day. You'll like Helen, our therapist, and once the pain in your leg subsides Sister will put you in a wheelchair with an extended leg-piece, which will give you much more freedom. You'll be able to propel yourself about, get into the day-room which is shared with the men next door. There's a widescreen TV in there so you can watch your favourite programmes, added to which there's your radio, and you'll have visitors, I'm sure.'

'I'll have to put a cloth over that...' she grimaced at her leg '...or my mother will keel over. She can't stand gruesome sights.'

'You'll have a bed cradle,' Anna promised, glad to see her cheering up.

'Yeah, right.' Kate watched the three of them walk over to the ward desk on their metal-free, easily moving legs. Did they know how lucky they were?

'It might be a good idea to move the two young fillies together,' Clive said, as they proceeded down the ward. He meant, move Margaret, the amputee, up beside Kate, and Mrs Hilton down by the doors, a suggestion that didn't find favour with Anna. She was just about to say so when he added, even more to her chagrin, 'Old Mrs Hilton won't mind.'

'I'm sorry, but I think she very well might.' Anna's voice was cool. 'She's only three days post-op and still anxious about herself. Put her down by the doors in Margaret's place and she'll think she's dying, or that something's gone wrong with her hip. Margaret will be crutch-walking any day now. If she wants to walk up here and talk to Kate then, fine, she can do so. I don't want Mrs Hilton disturbed.'

'I have to say I agree with Sister.' Daniel glanced at Clive.

'OK, OK, point taken.' Clive's rounded chin jerked. 'We all know Sister's word is law.' He gave an unpleasant laugh.

'We do, and in the matter of the ward management we take her advice.' Daniel's voice was firm to the point of censure, as he took himself out of the ward.

'Trust him to take your side,' Clive sneered as he, too, prepared to leave. 'Watch out he doesn't take other things as well, now that you're fancy-free!'

'Thanks for the warning, Mr Stone!' Anna tried to laugh off his words, but they returned to her an hour later when she was cycling home.

Did Daniel always take her side? She had never thought that he did. He merely respected her judgement, and she his, where the patients were concerned. He had come to the General from a post in London the same week she'd been appointed Sister so, in a sense, they'd been new together, and they'd got on right from the start. The barrier of rank was always there, of course, for even in these democratic days doctors and nurses, even doctors and ward sisters, kept to their own side of the fence.

Anna felt Daniel saw her as a colleague, which was how she wanted things to stay. They had never talked together all that much about anything other than work. They had never met outside the hospital, never been out on a date. There had never been any thought of it—there had always been Rob. I want him back, I want Rob back. The full awfulness of what he'd done, of what had happened between them, filled her up at times, right to the top, right over her head, as if she were drowning. Well, she couldn't drown now, she thought, fighting the feeling off, she was in heavy traffic. There was no need to end up under a bus—even Rob wasn't worth that.

Last week he had sent her the key of his house in Ditton Road—the house that was to have been their home, four-bedroomed and rather posh. It had been *his* home for two years, long before Anna had met him. It had been left to him by his maternal grandmother, fully furnished with all mod cons. He had lived there and commuted daily to his office in central London. Now he lived in London and the house was up for sale with Brett and Co.

The key had been sent to Anna so that she could collect her things from the house—movable things like ornaments and books, china and photographs. She had taken them there during their three months' engagement to set her stamp on the house, make it feel more homely, more like *her* home, too. It had given her such pleasure to see them in *situ*—her clock on the mantelshelf, her books on the shelves beside the fireplace, her lamp on the hall table. She could remember each time she had taken something, wobbling along on her bike.

Never had she thought—*never, ever had she thought*—
that Rob would let her down.

Well, he had, and now she must collect everything,
and the sooner the better. She'd go that night and get
it over with—cycle over after supper. Most of the
things would go in her backpack and the basket would
hold a lot, and it wouldn't be dark till half past nine.
Feeling slightly better, she made the turning into
Elvington Road where she and Julie rented the top of
a Victorian terraced house.

Julie worked office hours, so she wouldn't be home
until six. Still, no matter, she'd wait supper for her.
Putting a take-away lasagna in the oven, she changed
into jeans and a sweater, brushed out her hair and tied
it back in a ponytail. She was dragging her backpack
off the top of the wardrobe when she heard Julie come
in, thudding up the stairs in a rush and a flurry. Julie
never walked anywhere.

'How did it go? How did you get on?' Her buttercup
yellow hair—a shade lighter than Anna's—was in wild
disarray as she stood on the landing, looking search-
ingly at her friend.

'All right, I think… In fact, good on the whole,'
Anna admitted.

'Well, there you are, then. What did I say? You've
got guts, they'll see you through. But what are you
doing with that backpack? And what are we having to
eat? Is that Italian I smell?' She made a Bisto nose.

'It is, and it'll be ready in ten minutes.'

'Wicked, and I've got a bottle of plonk. I thought
we'd celebrate, you breaking the ice and all that.'

'Just what I need, although…' Anna laughed '…I'll
probably fall off my bike.'

'You're not going out again?' Julie looked round in surprise.

'Yes, I am, hence the backpack. I'm going to The Rowans to collect my things.'

'Oh, *Anna*.' Julie looked concerned. 'Must you go tonight?'

'Why not? I've got to get it over with some time— it may as well be tonight.'

'I'll come with you.'

'No, I don't want you to! Sorry, Ju, but that's how it is. It's something I must do on my own.'

'All right, then, do it.' Julie desisted at last. 'But if you're not back by nine I shall come looking for you.'

'I'll be back long before that.' Anna rattled cutlery on to the table. 'I'm not likely to want to hang about there, lost in what might have been.'

'I'm glad you didn't move in there with Rob. That would have made it even harder,' Julie remarked with her back to her friend as she rummaged for a cork-screw.

'And I'd have lost this comfortable pad with you,' Anna answered brightly. She and Rob had decided not to live together at The Rowans until they were married. This had been a whim on Rob's part, which Anna had gone along with. They had been lovers there, though, and it had been their haven—Rob's expression, not hers—but going there tonight would be painful, and she knew it. She had to go alone.

'Oh, go and get it over with,' Julie burst out, mentally cursing that control freak, Robert Dudley, whom she had never liked very much.

CHAPTER TWO

DITTON ROAD was nearly two miles away across town, and it was just on eight o'clock before Anna turned into its tree-bordered elegance, feeling breathless and slightly sick.

The first thing she noticed as she neared The Rowans was the 'For Sale' board at the gate, then she saw a car at the verge, with BRETT & CO., ESTATE AGENTS lettered along its side.

She dismounted and hung back a little, wondering what to do, for the car could only mean that Mr Brett was showing someone round. Surely it was very late in the day. Still, as she'd said herself, the evenings were long at this time of year, and would-be buyers would probably be at work during daytime hours. She decided she couldn't just burst in and interrupt any discussion. Perhaps if she waited a few minutes they'd come out and leave the coast clear. As she propped her bike against the wall she could see the roof of another car parked in the drive and screened by the privet hedge. So there *was* someone viewing, probably a whole family looking round, and she hated the thought of it. Rob and she should be living there now. It shouldn't have a bunch of strangers tramping in and out of the rooms.

Even as she thought this the front door opened, and she could see Mr Brett with his sharp black beard turned to someone in the hall. She stepped forward out of the shadows—after all, why not? There was no reason for her to skulk as though she had no right to be there. 'Good evening,' she called, her voice ringing out.

'Why, Miss Chancellor, hello!' John Brett came down the steps all smiles and shook hands with her. He was acquainted with her through her parents, and he guessed why she'd come. He had heard from his client—her erstwhile fiancé—that she had a key to the house, and would be collecting one or two items that belonged to her.

'You'll have come for your possessions, no doubt?' His gaze rested on her face—as pretty as a picture, took after her mother, wonderful hazel brown eyes. But Anna was looking beyond him towards the house, looking at who was about to emerge from the dimness of the hall. Perhaps it wasn't a buyer—perhaps it was Rob. Then her jaw dropped as a rangy figure appeared at the top of the steps, his dark, saturnine features mirroring her own astonishment. It was Daniel… *Daniel*…but what on earth was he doing here?

'Good Lord!' That was all she could manage as he joined her on the path.

'Are you house-hunting too? Are we rivals?' He was laughing to hide his surprise.

'Absolutely not.' She was quick to reply. 'Plainly you didn't know, but this is Rob's house. I'm here to collect some things that belong to me.'

'Well, I'm damned.' His mouth opened and shut. 'I had no idea! So this is where—'

'Certainly is.' Anna smiled and kept on doing so, making her facial muscles ache, her teeth go dry.

'Plainly you know one another?' a confused Mr Brett interposed.

'We're colleagues at the hospital,' Daniel informed
him, 'so I'll stay here, Mr Brett, and give Miss
Chancellor a hand. Thank you for showing me round
in what I'm sure is your leisure time. I'll be letting you
know what I decide within the next day or two.'

Mr Brett wagged his head and looked serious. 'We
have other parties interested,' he said. 'At this time of
year properties sell quickly, and this one's in prime
condition.'

'I agree. It is.' Daniel was watching Anna going up
the steps. The front door was ajar and she disappeared
inside the house. 'So I'll say goodnight,' he said more
firmly, and Mr Brett went off.

Anna was wishing she'd told Daniel she could manage, but as she hadn't she could hardly shut the door
behind her and leave him outside. The thing was, she
didn't want to make a fool of herself in his presence,
and she so easily might because the familiar smell and
feel of the house was beginning to get to her. How
many times had she rushed in here, straight into Rob's
arms? Why, even the stairs had a mocking voice of
their own—'You're never going to get over him, are
you? You'll never love anyone else.'

'I don't mean,' Daniel was saying behind her, 'to
butt in in any way but, on a practical level, if there's
anything you want lifted…'

'It's all small stuff—bits and pieces, not furniture.
I'll start in here.' Anna went into the sitting-room, then
gave a little gasp. Two tables had been pushed together
and laid out on them were what she had come for—
every one of her things. There was even a typed sheet
listing them, with a place for her to sign. Trust Rob to
be meticulous—he wasn't a lawyer for nothing. Of
course, he could have been trying to spare her the or-

deal of walking all over the house, but a list was the limit. Even so, she signed it, resisting the temptation to put at the end, 'Satisfied, I trust?'

'You may as well come in,' she called out to Daniel, who was inspecting a picture in the hall. 'Everything has been put in here, which saves me looking round.' Roughly she opened the backpack and began piling everything in.

Daniel stopped her. 'You're going to break something. Let me help, for goodness' sake!' He took the pack from her, glancing at her face.

'Oh, all right, if you like.' She walked over to the window and stood with her back to him. He had wondered about all this impedimenta—he laid a Poole pottery vase in the pack—when he had been touring the house with John Brett, but hadn't asked what it was. The typed inventory which he could see on the table was sensible, he supposed, but in the absence of any kind of note it was a cool way of doing things. He felt the stirrings of anger on her behalf as he finished his packing at last.

'I'll carry this lot out.' He retained his hold on the pack as she reached to take it from him. 'If you want to look round, or anything, I'll be waiting in the car.'

'I don't need to look round,' she replied shortly, 'but if *you* want a final tour… I mean, if you're thinking of buying…'

'Not now, that can wait!' Still holding her pack, he began to walk to the door. Again she resisted, pulling at the pack. 'It's meant to go on my back. I'm cycling. I've left my bike by the gate.'

'And what about the books?' She was holding a leaning tower of them against one hip.

'They're to go in the basket—it's a large one.' She saw him shake his head.

'You'll never manage, never balance—not on a bike. You'll come off in traffic.'

'I won't, I assure you!' She looked defensive.

Again he shook his head. 'Anna, I can't possibly be responsible for letting you go off laden like that. I'll put everything in the car, tie your bike on the roof and run you home!'

'Tie the bike on your car?' She gaped at him. He couldn't be serious. His car—an Oxford green BMW—was the last word in elegance.

'Relax, it's my brother's car,' he told her, laughing. 'A battered but roadworthy Metro, complete with roof rack. There's a heap of junk in the boot—bound to be rope, or string or straps. Anyway, I'll fix it, and get you home in one piece. Otherwise, decent chap that I am, I won't sleep tonight!'

Put like that, she had little choice but to accept, thank him and relinquish the books, which he put in the car behind the hedge, along with the bulky pack. Fetching the bike, she helped him hoist it aloft and sort out some ties from the boot. Once in place and firmly fixed, they set off towards the town.

It was a little, Anna thought as they left Ditton Road, like drawing away from one's past, except, of course, that the past couldn't be dismissed so easily. It had a habit of returning, of creeping up, of whispering in one's ear, 'I'm still here, you know. I'm not far away. I'm not for forgetting yet.' Even so, if only temporarily, she was aware of feeling relieved, jolting along in the little car which, despite its battered appearance and the rattling bike on top, was doing its job well. Yes, she was...she was relieved.

'We're making good progress,' Anna said, feeling she couldn't stay silent. Daniel was putting himself out to help her, and there must have been other things he'd far rather have done.

'My car,' he explained, as they breasted Magdalene College bridge, 'has an engine fault so I've been loaned this for the next few days. James and I help one another out, that's what brothers are for.'

'I suppose so.' They exchanged quick smiles.

'Have you got a brother or sister?' he asked.

'No, I'm a spoiled only child!'

'I've a married sister in Cornwall, a little older than me. She has three kids—little devils, not that I see them much. There are thirteen years between James and I. He's just finishing his first year at Corpus Christi College, reading law.'

Like Rob did, Anna thought, making the comment that having siblings must be great. Their conversation lapsed as they entered the town centre. Dusk was falling, but the air was still warm, redolent of mown grass and the river, less romantically of traffic fumes. Lights were springing up in college doorways, old-fashioned lamps gleamed palely in ancient courtyards, while the streets were alive with a mixture of 'town' and 'gown' all out to enjoy themselves.

'You've missed the turning,' she told him sharply, as he continued past the roundabout into the hubbub of Trinity Lane.

'Not missed it—ignored it.' He smiled, the car now at crawling pace. Students were passing *en masse* on their cycles, so close that their elbows bumped against the windows which were dark with their moving shapes. 'Once we're through this scrum we're going to the Red Lion for a drink. Both of us have had a long hard day.' And you need a brandy, if I can get it down you, he finished inside his head as they saw daylight at last and turned into the less jam-packed St Mary's Square.

Anna made a protest, then decided against it because clearly he was being kind. Also—there was no doubt about it—being looked after was growing on her. The only thing was, jeans and a sweater, with a fleece jacket on top, was hardly the gear for the Red Lion, unless they were going to the bar, of course. It was clear they weren't, however, for once through the entrance lobby he propelled her through into the cocktail bar, where he ordered a tonic for himself and a brandy and soda for her.

'I'm being spoiled,' she said, sipping her drink and feeling better by the minute. Daniel was making an effort, being nice to her. She knew why and didn't resent it as she would have done with some people, and wondered why that was. He was a doctor, of course, and that might have something to do with it. She looked at him over her glass, taking him in piece by piece, scarcely aware of doing so. Inevitably she compared him with Rob, who'd been fair with chiselled features and an overall neatness—a good-looking man, in fact.

This man, this Daniel, was different. He suited his name. He looked like a Daniel with his thick dark hair worn just a shade too long, his grey eyes fringed with black lashes, his big mouth the smiling kind. She looked at his hands—long-fingered and strong, with blunt well-kept nails.

She was lost in a reverie, and jumped when he said, 'We don't usually have time for personal scrutiny, do we, Anna?'

'Sorry to stare.' She collected herself. 'I do it all the time. You see, I sketch a bit, draw and paint. I was getting you into perspective. Sorry if I was rude.'

'You weren't. I didn't mind.' He smiled, and his eyes narrowed in amusement, or maybe he was getting *her* into perspective. 'Sadly,' he continued, 'I have no excuse for staring at you, other than the obvious one!'

She let that pass. So he could flirt, could he? How little she knew about him. Off duty he was practically a stranger, she realised with a shock.

'Any artistic bent must be a positive antidote to the trials of ward management, but what I'm wondering is when you have the time to indulge it,' he said seriously.

'Evenings and, occasionally, weekends. It's easier in the summer, and I'll have more time now, being un-attached. Having someone else to consider and do things with takes up a lot of time!' Fired by the brandy, this was easy to say, and she even managed to laugh.

'You need friends and fun, even so.' She noticed he didn't laugh back. His eyes were looking straight into hers, sending out messages, telling her that he found her lovely, and she felt her heart skip a beat. For goodness' sake, this couldn't be happening, she didn't *want* it to happen.

'Are you going to buy Rob's house?' she asked him all in a rush.

His face changed, and he set down his glass. 'I don't think so, no. It's farther from the hospital than I thought. I hadn't realised that Ditton Road was such a long one.'

'Nearly a mile. It runs right through to the Fellingdon Bypass.'

'So Mr Brett told me.'

'There'll be other properties coming onto the market. This is a good time of year to be looking.' She badly wanted to know why he wanted a whole house. Most unmarried registrars lived in flats, and he'd already got one of those—a very classy one, so Pam Fiske had told her, in a block called Maitland House.

'I'm looking for a property spacious enough for James and I to share,' he said, as though reading her mind. 'He's had an appalling run of digs so far and, as he and I have always got on, it seems a good idea. We shall each want our own quarters, though. We each need privacy.'

'Oh, I can see that, yes,' Anna said very nearly light-heartedly. A place for his brother and he to share. Well, of course, that made sense. 'There, now.' She smiled, and put out a feeler. 'I thought you were getting married, or something like that!'

'I've been married, and it's not the kind of commitment I mean to repeat,' he said, so coldly that she felt well and truly snubbed...appalled at herself for having tried to quiz a man like him. She wanted to apologise, but a surprised exclamation was all she could get out because she *was* surprised, and that, as well as discomfiture, kept her silent for a time. It was he who adroitly guided their talk on to safer, general lines.

They discussed what was on at the Arts Theatre in Keys Lane, which often had top-class shows before they went on to the West End. 'You can't, even so, beat seeing a show *in* London,' Daniel said. 'The very fact of where you are, the whole atmosphere, lends a special buzz.'

'That's very true,' Anna agreed. She and Rob had seen one or two shows during their six months together, she meeting him at Temple underground station, but already that seemed years ago.

Daniel asked her if she would like another drink, but she shook her head, saying that she ought to be on her way, 'otherwise, Julie, my flatmate, will be sending out a search party all along Ditton Road!'

'Wasting police time!'

'Exactly!' She laughed, relieved to see that the false note she'd struck earlier on seemed to have done no harm.

As she stood up he helped her into her jacket, lifting her ponytail to lie outside it, surprised by its silky weight. She felt the slight movement—a practised one, too. He knew how to handle a woman. Well, of course he did. He'd been married, hadn't he, and goodness knew what besides?

'Thanks,' she said in a muffled voice, and then they were off, walking over the green carpet scrolled with dragons' heads. It was as they were about to pass through the doors that they ran straight into Clive Stone who was coming in with a nurse from Intensive Care whom Anna knew by sight.

'Well, well, a meeting of the clans!' Clive's grin flashed out, 'You know Rosalie, don't you?' He thrust his companion forward. 'What a small world it is!'

The usual pleasantries were exchanged, and the two moved off into the cocktail lounge. 'And that, of course, means,' Anna said as she got into the Metro, 'that it'll be all over the unit tomorrow that you and I were out together.'

'Does that bother you?' Daniel's head came close as he fastened his safety belt and switched on the lights in one deft movement.

'A little.' Anna watched the beams of light swing as he turned the car roadwards.

'Can't say it does me, not in the least,' he said promptly and cheerfully, then, accelerating cautiously across the square, asked her if she'd made any friends during her two weeks at The Avenue Clinic.

'I wouldn't say friends, but they were a good crowd,' she said. 'I enjoyed being there. Nursing in the private sector isn't so rushed—there was time to spend with colleagues as well as with the patients. It was a completely fresh scene, and I'm glad I made the effort. I couldn't have spent that fortnight twiddling my thumbs in the flat.'

Plenty of people could and would have, Daniel thought, but didn't say so. As he started to slow to make the turn into Elvington Road he asked her if they could meet up one evening—have a meal out, take in a film, perhaps, or a show, whichever she wanted.

She was flattered but at the same time panicked into refusing. She didn't want to. *No way*, she simply didn't want it. 'Daniel, thanks, it's a nice thought, but I'd rather not. I don't mean to be rude but…'

'Too soon for you, I expect.'

She told him it was, knowing full well that wasn't the whole of the story. She didn't want to take the first step into a relationship for ages, certainly not into a relationship that might make a difference to her work. It had been devastating, losing Rob, but she'd had her work to turn to, like a shelter from the storm of her feelings, like a comforting hand to hold. Daniel was a friend *at* work. He was part of her working life and she didn't want to change the status quo—she liked it just as it was. Anyway, she thought as she stole a glance at him, he didn't seem at all put out. 'Don't worry about it. It was just a thought,' he said as he drew up outside her flat and squeaked the handbrake on.

The thought came to Anna, as she prepared to get out, that Rob, in a similar situation, would have reacted very differently. Rob hadn't liked being refused. Any whiff of rejection, however gently voiced, sent him into a sulk for hours, leaving *her* feeling guilty when it should have been the other way round. Daniel, now, was perfectly cheerful about it, even to the extent of humming a tune as he opened her door for her.

The house, slate-roofed, bay-windowed and porched, exactly the same as its neighbours, was late Victorian, solid and well built, and had a homely air. Elvington Road had the original streetlamps which had once been gas, and even now, electrically lit, they bore no resemblance to the modern-day cement stalks with their greenish, sodium flares. Daniel was looking about him appreciatively.

'Nice area,' he observed, just as Julie, having heard the car, came out of the front door.

'I was just getting worried.' She lifted the latch of the gate, while old Mrs Pelly on the ground floor parted her curtains to look out. Anna introduced Daniel to Julie, and the two shook hands.

'You must blame me for the lateness.' Daniel reached into the car for the books. 'I took your friend for a drink. She didn't want to come…' He paused significantly, then added, 'But as she was in the car at the time I was able to call the shots!'

'Good for you!' Julie had a good look at him as he put the books in her arms.

'Where does this go?' He angled the bike.

'Oh, we take it inside. Mrs Pelly doesn't mind.'

Anna took it from him. 'Thanks for everything, Daniel.' She was all for him going now.

Julie, though, wanted to keep him. 'How about a coffee,' she suggested, 'before you hit the road?'

'Well, thanks, but, no, thanks.' He was looking at Anna wheeling her bike up the path. 'I'd better get back. Things to do, you know. Good to meet you, Julie.' And then he was off, turning the car in the lamp-lit road, then driving down it with a parting wave of his hand.

'You never told me he was like *that*,' Julie enthused once they were in the house. 'He has the sexiest voice I've ever heard, and he's so romantic-looking!'

'You'll be telling me next that he's drop-dead gorgeous!'

'That's exactly how I see him.'

'You couldn't have seen much, out in the street.'

'Well, you wouldn't let me ask him in or, rather, you wouldn't let *him* say yes. Is he married, or anything?'

'Not married now, but he has been, I gather.' Anna followed Julie's bobbing short skirt up the stairs to their flat.

'How did you come to run into him tonight, or had you arranged to do so?'

There was no way Julie was going to leave the subject, so Anna put her in the picture after they'd dumped everything down on the landing and repaired to the sitting-room.

'Nice of him to help.' Julie looked reflective.

'I thought so, yes.'

'And he took you for a drink.'

'I told you, yes.' Anna held her breath at this point, for she knew what was coming next.

'I bet he asked you out, didn't he—again, I mean?'

'He did, but I'm not going, Julie. I like him a lot, but at the moment I don't want to even so much as think about a relationship. I just can't. The thought of it panics me. I've lost confidence, I suppose. Anyway,' she added in the silence that followed, 'Daniel didn't mind.'

'Maybe not.' Julie was through in the kitchen, filling the kettle. 'A man like him isn't likely to find it hard to get a date.' Getting no reply and relenting a little, she came back to give her friend a hug. 'Anyway, Anna, old duck, you've done brilliantly today. You've faced that crowd at the hospital, been to the love-nest and collected your things *and* been brought home by a ravishing stranger. Now, for starters, that can't be bad!'

Julie, Anna reflected in bed that night, was the best sort of friend to have. She was supportive and encouraging—more like a sister, in fact. They had met at the river swimming club and had been sharing the flat for three years. Before then it had been let to two schoolteachers who'd retired to live on the coast.

When Anna had got engaged and her wedding date had been fixed, Julie had known she'd have to take in someone else because she wouldn't have been able to pay the whole rent herself. Despite Anna's urgings, however, she had kept delaying making enquiries. 'I'll do it when you've actually tied the knot, and not before,' she'd said.

And thank heavens she'd taken that line, Anna mused as she switched off her light. If she hadn't, it would have been back to the hotel for me, living with Mum and Dad. That would have been all right...well, of course it would...but even so, especially now that I'm not being married, I want to live my own life.

CHAPTER THREE

ANNA was on lates next day, which meant she was on duty from twelve-thirty to nine p.m. It was a very different day from yesterday, too, being windy with a fine rain. Not that she cared about the weather—she had other things on her mind. Divesting herself of her raincoat and slipping her feet into a dry pair of ward shoes, she walked swiftly down the corridor, to be met by Daniel, who was coming out of one of the side-wards, accompanied by a second-year nurse.

'A new admission obviously,' she said before he could speak, '*and* an emergency as you've commandeered my side-ward!' She was joking in a forced kind of way, trying to dispel a tinge of embarrassment at the sight of him after last night. She quickly forgot her own feelings, however, when he told her what had happened.

'It's your landlady, Mrs Pelly,' he said. 'She was admitted via Cas. a couple of hours ago with a fractured femur. It seems she fell in the shopping mall. Someone from Boots called an ambulance.'

'Oh, dear!' Anna stared back at him. 'Oh, poor Mrs Pelly! I saw her go off soon after breakfast. She was going to buy a new hat for her great-niece's wedding and have lunch out afterwards. Oh, dear, what a thing to happen!' Dismissing the nurse, she and Daniel went into the office together.

'She's had Fortral by injection,' he said, 'and been put on skin traction for the time being. She's shocked,

38

of course, but clear-headed—doesn't seem confused.'
He handed over the casualty card and hastily compiled
notes, adding that as the patient had eaten breakfast,
surgery was out till next morning.

'Will you do it? Will you be operating?' Anna was
looking at the notes.

'Yes, I've got her on my list for half-eight, so nil by
mouth as from suppertime tonight.' Daniel perched on
the edge of the desk.

'I must go in and see her.'

'She's already asked for you, *and* she's told Nurse
Piers that she likes to be called ''Mrs Pelly'' and not
''Edith'', if you please!'

Anna smiled automatically, but inside she was
vexed. 'All the staff,' she said, 'have been told to ask
before using first names. Some of the older patients
don't like it, which in a way I can understand. They
take the old-fashioned line that familiarity breeds con-
tempt.'

'Permission to be friendly has a lot going for it,'
Daniel remarked cryptically. Anna couldn't see his ex-
pression as he was looking at Mrs Ventnor's notes and
X-ray report which were lying on the desk.

'I'll be along again around teatime,' he told her, 'to
see Mrs V. and her husband. Her radiculogram shows
a severe disc protrusion between vertebrae four and
five. Both Sir Guy and I feel that a laminectomy is the
only answer now. I've explained this to Mrs Ventnor,
but she's very anti-surgery. She wants to talk it over
with her husband when he visits this afternoon. *If* she
signs the consent form I'll get her on tomorrow's list.'

They moved out of the office, Daniel standing back
for Anna to pass him. 'You in good order today?' he

asked, his eyes taking in her heavy gold bun, raised up high today, showing the nape of her neck.

'Great, yes, never better!' She turned to smile at him, taking him unawares for a second, making him draw in his breath...

'That's what I like to hear,' he said throatily, then made off at speed, his white coat, hanging neatly for once, banging against his legs.

Edith Pelly was relieved to see Anna and her pale, anxious face brightened at the sight of her. 'Oh, Miss Chancellor—oh, sorry, I should say ''Sister'', shouldn't I? Look what I've done! I fell, coming out of the shopping mall—missed one of the steps! I knew I'd broken a bone, the pain was simply terrible. Even now the slightest movement makes it start up again!'

'Yes, I know, Mrs Pelly. I've heard what happened, and I couldn't be more sorry.' Anna sat down and took one of her neighbour's hands, careful not to jar the bed.

The old lady's injured leg had a long splint bandaged against it, the splint ending in a length of cord which passed over a pulley. There were weights at the distal end of the cord, hanging down like a pendulum. Her bed end was raised to give the required stretch, or pull, on the limb to stop it from going into spasm prior to surgery.

'What will happen next, dear?' Mrs Pelly looked anxious again. 'They did tell me but I couldn't take it in, not all of it anyway.' Her words came thickly and more slowly now, due to the analgesia she'd been given.

'Well, your leg will be mended down in Theatre to-morrow under a general anaesthetic. It'll be done by metal-plating, making it safe and strong. You won't have to have it in plaster, but you'll have a wound in your thigh and a little tube, which we call a drain, to take any fluid away. When you wake up you'll be in a little ward downstairs till your blood pressure and pulse have been taken, then you'll come back here where we'll look after you till you're ready to walk out of the doors. It won't be so bad, you'll see.' Anna gave her hand a squeeze.

'What will happen to the house?' She was nearly asleep.

'Julie and I will look after the house. Now, I'm going to ring your daughter, and let her know what's happened.'

'They asked me downstairs who my next of kin was. I told them it was Doris...at Ballaters Store in Ipswich, in the china and glass department. You'll remember her from coming to the house once or twice, but I don't think—' the old lady looked worried '—she'll like being disturbed at work.'

'For something as important as this she won't mind. Now, you try and get some rest.' Anna moved quietly out of the side-ward and into her office next door.

Doris Court, as Anna remembered a few minutes later, whilst speaking to her over the phone, had a powerful voice, quite unlike her gentle mother's. 'Broken her hip, you say?'

'Yes, I'm afraid so. She'll have surgery tomorrow. Meanwhile, we're keeping her as comfortable as possible. She knows I'm ringing you. There won't be a lot of point in visiting her tomorrow, Mrs Court, because she'll be asleep all day, but on Thursday I'm sure she'll want to see you. Our visiting time is from two o'clock right through till seven, so if you're travelling—'

'Most old people,' Doris interrupted, 'break their

hips at some time or other. I've heard it's called the "inevitable fracture" in people over seventy-five.'

'Well, yes,' Anna agreed, somewhat nonplussed.

'And it's not as if it's life-threatening, is it?'

'No.' Anna drew in her breath. 'Even so, it's not a slight happening. The degree of shock to someone of your mother's age is very considerable.'

'She's eighty-five.'

'So I saw from her notes.'

'Still, I'm sure she's in good hands. I'll be along on Sunday—best to leave it till then. Thursday's my half-day, when I've always got a lot on. I dare say, by Sunday, she'll be up and walking around.'

'Mrs Court.' Anna was trying her best to keep the ice out of her voice. 'I think you're confusing a broken hip with a hip replacement. Your mother will be out of bed quite soon, but she won't be fully mobile and walking unaided for several weeks.'

'Like I say, I'll be along on Sunday.' Doris Court wasn't giving an inch.

'I'll give her your love, shall I?'

'Of course, yes, do that, and thank you for letting me know.' The phone was replaced so abruptly that Anna was left with hers still held to her ear.

'The daughter from hell!' she said explosively, re-turning the receiver to its rest just as her second-in-command, Jane Scott, put her head round the door.

'Are you going up to lunch, Anna, or shall I get you a sandwich?' she asked.

'She's coming up to lunch with me.' Pam Fiske's determined bulk appeared behind Jane. 'I've heard of these snatched lunches of yours, Anna, and I don't ap-prove.'

Over lunch—fish, as it was Tuesday—Pam made the

point that a little bird had told her Anna had been out with 'our Daniel' the night before.

'A little bird by the name of Clive Stone,' Anna said unsurprised. 'We ran into him at the Red Lion, where I was being treated to a drink. I met Daniel up at Rob's house.' Briefly she explained the circumstances. 'So you see it wasn't a question of being out with him. It was in no sense a date.'

'Still…' Pam pushed a piece of batter to the side of her plate. 'He took the trouble to help you and fortified you afterwards.'

'He's a caring type, he'd have done it for anyone.'

'Not a chance! He might have run just "anyone" home, but he wouldn't have taken her for a drink and spent extra time with her. And why are you so fey about it? Surely it's good for the old self-esteem to have a personable male lusting for your company?'

'It's too soon,' Anna protested.

'The sooner the better! If Robert had died, instead of dumping you, then, I agree, it would have been too soon, but he's alive and kicking with someone else, and you must do the same. It's a little like getting back into the saddle when a horse has thrown you off.'

'The two issues are entirely different and my self-esteem doesn't need bolstering. It's not as low as all that.' Anna was slightly shocked. There were times when Pam didn't so much make a point as hammer it home. Even so, she was right in some ways, she conceded as she made her way back to her ward. It *had* been confidence-building to have Daniel dancing attendance on her, not to mention asking her out.

She hadn't told Pam about the latter because she'd only have gone on and on about Anna having turned him down. She was still glad she'd said no, but she had liked being asked—had liked it so much that she couldn't help hoping he might ask again.

He didn't. Over the next two weeks he was just as friendly, just as affable, and they got on just as well within the ward environment. However, they seldom spoke of matters that didn't concern the patients, apart from remarks about the weather and the traffic in the town, and the occasional exchange of day-to-day pleasantries which didn't lead to anything. That didn't disappoint Anna exactly, although it caused her to wonder if she might have passed up on something enjoyable for no good reason.

Mrs Pelly progressed very slowly. Now in her second week post-op she was persuaded to sit in a chair for short periods, which she didn't like at all, complaining of pain in her wound and general malaise. 'It'll be another month before I can discharge her,' Daniel said, 'unless it's to a nursing home where she can be mobilised gradually.'

'Julie and I can keep an eye on her when she gets home.' Anna was watching the physiotherapist helping the old lady back to bed.

'But neither of you is there during the day, though, are you?' Daniel's voice had an edge of impatience. 'Perhaps her daughter can get time off for the first two weeks of discharge.'

But Mrs Court couldn't, or wouldn't, and she made that very plain. 'Keep her in here, or send her to a convalescent home. She needs professional help.' Doris had visited only twice during the fortnight, bringing nothing with her in the way of flowers or fruit—just a small tube of Murray Mints, which she seemed to think adequate.

Generally speaking, the patients' stay on the ortho

wards was several weeks, and sometimes months. Most adapted to this, accepting the hospital routine and gradually being mobilised. Each and every one of them, though, looked forward to visiting time, which was why, with a little prompting from Anna, Julie made her appearance three or four evenings a week at Mrs Pelly's bedside.

Mrs Hilton, Kate Denver's bed-neighbour, was discharged on Thursday into the care of her husband, who couldn't wait to take this on. Mrs Ventnor, still on flat bed-rest after her laminectomy, was having a little moan again, demanding to know how she was—had her operation been a success or was she doomed again?

'I think,' Daniel said, after Edith Pelly's fourteenth day post-op, 'that she could be helped out of bed, just to stand—wearing her corset, of course, but not to sit, not yet at this delicate healing stage.'

'On the whole she's being a better patient than I thought.' Anna poured him a second cup of tea. It was five o'clock, and he looked gaunt and tired after a day in Theatre. She wondered if he'd found a suitable house for himself and his brother yet, but didn't like to ask. Then she took courage and did so. 'Any luck with the house-hunting?' she said.

He shook his head. 'I'm afraid not. The Rowans was the nearest I've come to finding what we want.' He stirred his tea and sipped it thoughtfully before he added, 'Actually, it's still on the market, Mr Brett told me yesterday. It seems he's had offers for it but not near enough to the asking price.'

'Rob is likely to hold out for the full price, I can tell you that,' Anna said flatly. 'Not that I've heard from him. I haven't.' It seemed important to make that clear. 'But I know how he is about money.'

'It's too far from the hospital for me, and not all that convenient for James, so I must rule it out and be done with it.' Daniel got to his feet. 'Thanks for the tea—a life-saver! Now I've got to meet Trevor Rees, the neuro reg over in Athelstone. We've got a patient in there on halo traction—a cranial injury case. He should be in the neuro ward, but it's the old cry of no beds.'

A sharp rap at the door at this point heralded the arrival of Mrs Parsons, the principal nursing officer, who had come about empty beds. 'I see the second of your side-wards is free.' She looked at Anna first, then included Daniel in her sweeping regard, as though daring him to disagree.

'Another emergency admission?' Anna tried to hide her dismay, for she hadn't enough nurses as it was.

'A fractured femur case being transferred from the Duchy of Cornwall Infirmary tomorrow. She's a Mrs Crowther, a resident of Seftonbridge—fell while on a coaching holiday in Bedruthan ten days ago. She's in her early fifties, has done well post-op and is fit to be moved, but she'll need to be barrier-nursed for a few days to rule out hospital cross-infection. And, yes, sister—' Mrs Parsons hadn't missed Anna's horrified look '—I do know that makes extra work and that you're already tightly stretched, but I've been in touch with the nursing agency and they've promised to send us a Grade D nurse by tomorrow afternoon. Depending on the traffic, Mrs Crowther should arrive here in time for lunch. Her notes will accompany her in the ambulance.'

'I see. Thank you.' Anna made a note on her pad.

'Shouldn't you be off duty?' Mrs Parsons addressed her again.

'I'm just on the point of going, Mrs Parsons.'

'And how about you, Mr Mackay? Is life treating you tolerably well?' Barbara Parsons homed in on Daniel, her expression softening.

What is it to be male and good-looking, Anna thought, watching as Daniel returned the smile, assuring her that he was fine.

'And that's one brisk lady,' he commented when she had gone.

'Well, let's hope she was brisk with the agency and that the promised nurse will turn up.' Anna was talking half to herself as she set the teatray on one side. 'Her first job will be to take swabs from Mrs Crowther and rush them off to the lab. Barrier-nursing is something I can do without, even with extra help.'

'Bad luck, though, to have an accident on holiday,' Daniel observed, 'but she'll have had good care at the Duchy Infirmary—that's where my sister had her kids. She couldn't speak too highly of it.'

'If it's that good we're unlikely to have the patient turning up with bed-sores, which will be something to be thankful for,' Anna said wearily, rubbing the small of her back. Watching her, Daniel was tempted to say that she needed to let go a bit—to allow a little fun into her life, which he could provide if only she'd let him, but at the moment he knew she wouldn't. Her thoughts and inclinations were still bound up with the Dudley bloke…him and his house, and his printed inventory. He swore inside his head.

After he'd gone, every bit as briskly as Mrs Parsons, Anna handed over to Jane Scott, went in to say goodnight to Mrs Pelly who was reading the *Argus*, then made tracks for home.

The house, during the past two weeks, had felt entirely different without Mrs Pelly pottering about downstairs. Anna missed the sound of *The Archers* every night at seven, and later, just before the old lady retired, the louder sound of *Crimewatch* on TV, which Mrs Pelly loved to watch. 'We all need to keep alert, dear, in these troubled days.'

Mounting the stairs to a silent flat, Anna remembered that Julie and her boyfriend, Sean, were going up to Town this evening and wouldn't be home until late. She, Anna, was going to have dinner with her parents at the hotel, but first she wanted to get out of her working garb and listen to the news. It was still only six-thirty when she left the house in a pink linen dress and cream blazer, her gold hair hanging loose. She walked up the road to its blind end, which gave out onto the water-meadows and the winding river bank.

The evening was warm, more like summer than the end of May. There were punts and other craft on the river, couples strolled hand in hand and a lark sang from high up, dropping like a stone to its nest. It seemed to Anna as she walked along the towpath that the whole world was coupling up, all living creatures were mating and nesting. As for me, I'm like the Cat that walked on its Wild Lone, she thought. Why is it that the long, light evenings are the loneliest time of all? It's because, her wise inner voice told her, that's when you've got time to think. During the day you're working and your own state of mind has to take a back seat.

A punt glided by, poled by a tall youth in khaki shorts. A girl lounged amongst its cushions, eating a chocolate bar. Rob and I never took a boat out, Anna thought. She turned to watch the punt as it continued downstream, making for the boatyard and sheds. But, then, I never knew Rob in summer—we didn't meet until nearly November. How amazing to think that this time last year she hadn't known of his existence. How could only six months of knowing and cut-off make such a wounding gap?

The stone bridge spanning the river just beyond the bathing huts was peopled with undergraduates, eating burgers and fries from a mobile shop on the bank. A ghetto-blaster was blaring out music and a black and white dog, most likely belonging to the burger man, was raising its leg against a bag. A youth balanced on the parapet wall. He whistled as Anna passed. She was tempted to tell him his antics were dangerous, for if he fell in where the river ran shallow he could easily break his neck. Still, there it is, she thought, gaining the opposite bank at last. If I warn him he'll laugh and do it all the more. She wondered if she'd been as mad as that during her student days. Quite possibly she had, although she couldn't recall dancing on bridge parapets.

Walking a little more swiftly, she soon came within sight of the hotel, grey-walled and slate-roofed, set amid lush green lawns. Two-storeyed, with forty guest-rooms, it had once—prior to the Second World War—been a girls' preparatory school.

Anna's parents were in the garden, talking to a group of guests. Her father, catching sight of her, broke away and came to meet her—a big burly man in a tight dinner jacket—and enveloped her in a hug. 'Anna, darling, you came the river way, then?' He moved her back and looked into her face.

'I needed some fresh air.'

'You all right?'

'I'm fine.'

Her mother joined them, slender in green. Her hair

was the same bright colour as Anna's but cut short to frame her face. 'Hello, sweetie, lovely to see you. We thought you'd abandoned us!'

'Course not. Sorry, Mum.' Enveloped in a perfumed embrace, Anna could see that the dining-room was busy, the glassed-in veranda as well. 'Looks like you've got a full house,' she commented.

'Every room taken, all ready for next week's celebrations.' Her mother was referring to the May Balls and revels which, according to University tradition, were held during the first week in June.

Over a cold meal, eaten in the family flat, parents and daughter exchanged news, Anna recounting one or two amusing hospital incidents but steering well clear of anything to do with Robert, although she could tell that her mother was dying to ask if she was over him yet. Lois Chancellor, in the way of most mothers, wanted to see her daughter married.

It had taken considerable nagging on her husband's part to get her to send the unused wedding dress and veil to a local costumier's. 'For goodness' sake, Lois,' he'd said. 'Have a bit of sensitivity. Even if she marries someone else eventually, she won't wear the same damn dress!'

It was he who, shortly after eight-thirty, accompanied Anna down to the ground floor, taking a short cut through the dining-room to the lobby beyond. As he was on the verge of saying goodbye to her she glimpsed, back through the glass doors of the dining-room, Daniel, rising to his feet.

'Someone you know?' Edward Chancellor turned to follow her gaze.

'It's our ortho registrar, Daniel Mackay.' Her voice jerked a little.

'Good name!'

'Dad, stay and meet him.' Anna gripped his arm. 'He's coming out!'

A little surprised at her panicky plea, he did as she asked, and a few seconds later the two men were shaking hands. Daniel praised the restaurant, saying how much he'd enjoyed his meal. 'I'm here with my brother and his girlfriend…decided to give them a treat.'

'Good choice of venue!' Edward smiled.

Dad, Anna was thinking as he bent to kiss her good-bye, doesn't believe in false modesty, and good for him, I say.

He touched her cheek. 'Come again soon, poppet, and don't work too hard.' With a smile to Daniel, he turned and strode away in the direction of the kitchen garden to view his tomato plants.

'Anna.' Daniel put a hand on her arm. 'We're just at the coffee stage. Come and join us. I'd like you to meet James.'

'Oh, Daniel, I don't know.' She hesitated. 'I was just going home, and it's quite a walk…'

'I'll run you home afterwards. Rescue me, please. Save me playing gooseberry for the next half-hour!'

His hand firmed round her arm, which tingled in response. That should have warned her, if she genuinely didn't want to get involved, to say no and mean it. Instead, the gentle insistence pressure spurred her on to accept.

'Well, all right, then, thank you.' She smiled at him.

'That's more like it!' His hand moved to cup her elbow as they moved through the restaurant doors.

CHAPTER FOUR

SHAKING hands with Daniel's brother a few seconds later, Anna's first thought was how unalike they were, even counting the thirteen-year age gap. James was red-haired, with a fresh complexion and the brightest of blue eyes. His smile coming easily and readily, he was the friendly, extrovert type. His girlfriend, Rowena, very fair, had a limp appearance and a handshake to match, but her greeting was warm. 'Great to meet you, Anna. Daniel tells us you're a ward sister at his hospital.'

'She is, and a highly capable one.' Daniel looked round for another chair, which was already being rushed up.

Rowena poured the coffee, her enormous hoop earrings bobbing against her cheeks, her tongue stud well in evidence as she opened her mouth to gasp at the amount of sugar James was loading into his cup.

'Well, you know what they say, "Black as the devil and sweet as sin,"' he quoted, laughing at her.

'He'll die of blocked arteries before his name, won't he?' she appealed to Daniel.

'Knowing James, he'll probably get away with it and live to a hundred!' The two brothers exchanged grins.

Sipping her own near-sugarless coffee, Anna was tempted to tell Rowena that the stud would play havoc with her tooth enamel every time she chewed. Deciding that she didn't know her well enough to start dishing out advice, she merely asked, 'Are you two fellow students?' She smiled across at them.

'Yeah,' James answered, and for the first time Anna glimpsed a likeness to Daniel when he nodded and moved his hands. 'We're both reading law…just drawing to the close of our first academic year. Now we're all set for a bit of fun—'

'Which will start next week,' Rowena began, but was herself interrupted by James.

'Then it's the long vac when we scatter far and wide, although, actually…' he passed up his cup for more coffee '…I may spend part of my time here. Daniel and I are house-hunting.' He was speaking to Anna now. 'I don't want to be up in Scotland, thus giving him carte blanche!'

'Of course not,' Anna sympathised. 'You want a say in it, too.'

'The whole of the say, if he had his way!' Daniel feigned a baleful look.

Sibling affection was there all right, Anna observed. She felt a jab of envy. It would be good to have a brother, a close blood tie.

Rowena, tucking her pale hair behind her ears, proceeded to tell Anna that her parents lived in Singapore. 'I was educated in England—still am, of course, but I shall go home during the vac, and I'm looking forward to it. I'd like James to come with me, but I've had no luck so far.'

'James has a phobia about flying,' Daniel told Anna, when the party broke up and the two of them were walking to the car park. 'I don't think he's got another fear in his body, but flying is something he backs away from. Won't be persuaded to try.'

'Most people have *one* hidden fear,' she said. 'Mine's being buried alive.'

'Mine's being trapped—being caught up in circumstances from which there's no escape...or no honourable escape,' he said seriously as he unlocked the car. She would have liked to have asked him what he meant, but his expression put her off. Instead, she commented on the car.

'It's a real beaut,' she said.

'I like it.' He took the end of her seat belt and fastened it for her. 'Although I've had one or two teething problems, which I hope are now in the past.' He drove off, the movement so smooth that she felt as if they moved on air. 'And by the way...' He switched on the lights. 'I haven't had anything to drink so you're in safe hands.'

'I'm relieved to hear it.' She answered his smile, whilst awareness of him shot into her mind like an arrow, disturbing her calm. He was too attractive...too near...too close. One by one her defences went up. She swallowed and made a gurgling sound, like water going down the drain. He heard it—she was certain he did—*and* felt her tense withdrawal. His next words confirmed it.

'Anna, relax,' he said. 'I'm still the same old stiff-neck you see on the ward. I may find you attractive...*do* find you attractive...but I *can* control myself.'

Heat flooded her cheeks. Once again he glanced at her. 'Now I've embarrassed you.'

'Not all that much... Anyway, I'm easily embarrassed so don't let it worry you.'

They entered the busy part of the town and further verbal sparring was out. 'Seems to me Seftonbridge never sleeps.' Daniel negotiated a bus.

'It's not half past nine yet,' Anna pointed out. 'You wait until next week, then it literally doesn't sleep, not with May Balls going on until breakfast, the midnight boat races they call "The Bumps" and madrigals being sung under the bridges. Haven't you ever been here during May Week?' she asked.

'No, 'fraid not.' He was making the turn into Elvington Road. 'I'm looking forward to the experience.'

'I expect James is, too.' Anna was beginning to tense up again as they drew near to the house.

'James embraces all new experiences with open arms. He lives each day as though it's his last. I fear for him sometimes.' He pulled up at the house. Should she ask him in? Perhaps she should—it was only polite—but she could hardly offer him coffee, they were awash with the stuff. No, she wouldn't ask him. He wouldn't expect it, and if he did, well, tough luck.

That decided, she was just about to wish him goodnight when a flicker of movement at the upstairs flat window made her alert. She must have been mistaken. It must have been a shadow or a reflection, a trick of the light, but it came again. She saw a blurred face. Startled, she clutched Daniel's arm.

'There's someone up there…up in the flat. I saw a movement—there's someone there!'

'Are you sure?' He peered out of her window, leaning over her lap.

'Yes, I am, I'm sure. Someone's up there, and Julie's out so it's not her! No one else has a key. Someone's broken in!' She tumbled out onto the kerb.

'Wait!' He slipped over the seat and joined her. 'We'll go in together!' Up the short brick pathway they went. Daniel took the door-key and, going in in front of her, stepped from the porch into the hall just in time to see Mrs Pelly's daughter, Doris Court, coming down the stairs.

Anna stared at her blankly, initial relief that she wasn't a burglar giving way to annoyance that she'd been up in the flat. 'Were you looking for something upstairs, Mrs Court?' She was using her Ward Sister's voice, not that it had any effect on Doris who was smiling at them both and saying something about having heard their car.

'But what did you want? I noticed you were moving about in the sitting-room,' Anna persisted doggedly, not blocking the woman's path but confronting her nevertheless. Why should she get away with it?

'I came here to look over the whole house, to make sure it was all right, which is rather natural, don't you think, with my mother in hospital?' Doris, on the bottom stair, was Anna's height exactly.

'What is natural, Mrs Court,' Daniel put in politely, 'is that Miss Chancellor was alarmed to see a movement at her window. She thought, well, we both thought someone had broken in.'

'Your mother always asks when she wants to come upstairs for any reason at all.' Anna was still on the attack, getting crosser by the minute.

'But this evening you weren't here to ask, were you?' Doris smiled thinly, her eyes cool. 'Nothing of yours has been interfered with. You'll find everything just as you left it, including the kitchen tap which is dripping and needs a new washer.' She descended the step, forcing Anna back. 'I'm going back to Ipswich tonight so you'll have to excuse me if I'm going to catch my train.'

Daniel, drawing Anna to him, gave her arm a warning squeeze. Mrs Court sailed by and out of the door, leaving them to close it behind her, which Anna did, resisting a childish impulse to slam it hard. 'I had a lot more to say to her. I hadn't nearly finished!' Freeing her arm from Daniel's grasp, she darted up the stairs.

'I could tell that,' he said mildly, following her up, 'but perhaps it was best not to say too much.' Gaining the landing, he watched her darting in and out of the five different rooms.

'Why best?' she asked from the kitchen, where she was wrenching at the tap.

'Because…' he appeared in the doorway '…we don't know the whole of the score. Mrs Pelly may have given her a free hand to look round in her absence.'

'She wouldn't have asked her to poke round up here,' Anna said jerkily.

Turning round from the sink, all thoughts of Doris evaporated as she looked at Daniel in semi-shock… Looked at him standing there, standing on the green vinyl in her and Julie's kitchen, one hand on the jamb of the white-painted door, looking quite at home. How had he got here? *Up* here? Of course, he'd followed her in from the street—no, correction, he'd come in first because of Mrs Court, who could have been a burglar, and then he'd come up the stairs.

'Not grown two heads, have I?' he joked, but looked serious.

'No, of course not, I was miles away.' Dear heaven, what a lie that was. 'Thank you for coming in with me. I was really alarmed at first.'

'My pleasure,' he said, making no move to go, so now it was up to her.

'Would you like something?' she asked. 'I mean, tea

perhaps after all that coffee?' She managed to smile, but blushed as well.

'Tea would be just the job.'

'Well, look around, if you like, while I get it... You can hardly lose your way.'

'You don't mind?'

'No, I don't. You're not Mrs Court.' She plugged in the kettle, set a tray and took it into the sitting-room where she found him looking at one of her watercolours, which Julie had had framed. It was one of the upper river where it curved under the dipping trees near Byron's Pool.

'Is this one of yours?' He looked closely at the signature, and she switched on the centre light, drawing the curtains against the darkness outside.

'It is, but mostly I do black and white sketches. I'm not into the pretty stuff.'

'You have a lot of talent.' He didn't sound surprised, and she found that satisfying. She had *some* talent, she knew that, but to have it affirmed was great.

'I was never properly taught, I just sort of followed my instincts!' Looking at him as she passed him his tea, she thought how sketchable he was. His features were clear-cut and their irregularity made them interesting. She had once done a sketch of Rob, but he hadn't liked the result, saying that she hadn't captured the shape of the back of his head.

'I'm quite good,' she told Daniel immediately, 'at sketching people from memory. For instance, if I concentrated hard, I could get a good, sharp likeness of Mrs Court coming down the stairs.'

'With an elongated nose, perhaps?'

'Exactly!' she said, and they laughed over their tea and biscuits, any awkwardness between them gone.

'This house is bigger than one would think from the outside,' Daniel remarked presently.

'Yes, it runs a good way back. It's actually four-bedroomed, or would be in its natural state. Downstairs Mrs Pelly has had the old scullery turned into a cloaks and shower room. Even so, she's still got three rooms plus a kitchen.'

'The Victorians knew how to build.' Daniel's glance took in the high-coved ceiling. 'Is there a burglar alarm?'

'No, nor a smoke alarm either. Mrs Pelly is a bit of an ostrich where hazards are concerned. The Rowans, now, is a virtual Fort Knox. Rob is very security-conscious.' Anna pulled herself up short as she realised she was talking as though they were still together.

'Did you live there with him?' Daniel's question came so quickly that she was unprepared.

'No, I just visited there.' She met his eyes squarely. 'I kept on living here. Strictly speaking, when I got engaged Julie should have looked for someone else to share. I suggested she do so, but she wouldn't have it. Sufficient to the day, she said. Daniel...' Anna set down her cup. 'Wouldn't it be awful if Mrs Pelly decided to sell up? I mean, she's eighty-five, and she's had a fall. Perhaps that's why Mrs Court was here to-night—looking round with a view to putting it on the market.'

'I wondered that myself.' Daniel looked reflective, leaning back in his chair. 'And if you're on a furnished weekly let you could be turned out, just like that. That's why I didn't want you to blow your top just now.'

'Oh, *no!*' Anna banged a fist against her head.

'Don't worry, I may be entirely wrong.'

'Rob always said that we had no security of tenure, and of course he was right!'

'Strange how we keep seeming to get back to the subject of Robert Dudley!'

'Oh, I'm sorry, it's just…' Anna floundered.

'Am I allowed to ask what happened to split you up?' Daniel's eye was intent, but inviting, too, and kindly.

'He met an old girlfriend,' Anna said. 'Found he still loved her—well, more than me, at any rate—and he came to tell me so at the hotel. I was staying there with my parents that week. It was the Wednesday before the Saturday we were due to be married.' She finished abruptly, her eyes on Daniel. What was he going to say? He was looking at his cup, his expression unreadable.

There was a pause and then he said, 'That must have taken some doing.'

'What's that supposed to mean!' She was taken aback, shocked to the core. She'd been sure he would take her part.

'I mean that it couldn't have been easy for him, facing you like that. Some men would have phoned, or written, or simply bolted and left it at that.'

'Or even married me, I suppose,' she retaliated, 'and had the other girl as well…on the side!'

'I'm glad that didn't happen.'

'It never would have. Rob was too honest for that.' And now she had to praise him—she *had* to praise him. 'Why, he even,' she added, 'made a point of going through to my parents, and saying how sorry he was!'

'You still love him, don't you?'

'I'm trying not to, but, yes, I do. I can't turn the feeling off like that tap in the kitchen.' Tears prickled

under her lids. 'And we shouldn't be talking about him.
It's not right, it's not fair! You ask too many questions,' she flared. 'How would you like it if I asked
about your marriage break-up?'

'*Are* you asking?' he enquired calmly.

'Yes!'

'All right, I'll do my best to oblige.' He leaned forward a little, looking down at the teatray as though
searching for the right words.

'We were fellow students at St Mildred's, London.
We married at twenty-six when we were senior house
officers and pretty pleased with ourselves. The pleased
feeling died with marriage, and three years later we
were finished. It was almost as though, by marrying,
we had spoiled what we had. We decided to separate.

'Margot went abroad to practise medicine in South
Africa. She craved movement, excitement, adventure.
She was a wonderful doctor.' He smiled as though re-
calling this, and as Anna watched, her throat con-
stricted. He still cares for her, she thought, hearing him
say, as he looked up and met her eyes, 'We divorced
eighteen months ago, which was the last time I saw
her, just before she went abroad again.'

'Oh, dear. I'm sorry, I really am.' She swallowed
convulsively.

'Thanks, but, as my old father would say, I've put
it down to experience. One lives and learns. And now,
Sister Chancellor...' His smile was broad this time.
'It's high time I was on my way after so much revealing chat!'

She laughed, as he had intended, and closeness between them rushed back. They were just a little bit in
the same boat, she thought as she watched him bend,
pick up the tray and take it through to the kitchen. She

didn't get up for a minute. Something seemed to tell her to stay. Just for a minute, only a minute, sitting alone in the room, she had the strangest, weirdest feeling that they had been here before, here together in this house years and years ago, in a bygone age, when every brick had been new.

The feeling passed, leaving awe in its wake, and she felt she had nothing to say as they went downstairs, Daniel going first, giving her a foreshortened view of his head, shoulders and arm. One of his hands trailed down the polished bannister. When they reached the hall he turned. 'Thanks for the tea.' His voice sounded strained.

'Thanks for coming in, even though the intruder turned out to be Mrs Court!'

'Having her good look-round.' He laughed obligingly.

She could see him only dimly in the light that filtered down from the landing, so when he reached for her, when he drew her to him, she had only a split second's warning. Not that she cared, she was glad.... It was blissful to be held again, tight against a hard male body. Her arms went round his neck, bringing him even closer, as she slightly parted her legs.

But when he bent to kiss her, when he moved against her, realisation of what she was doing...of what was going to happen...made her panic, and struggle, and push against him. 'I'm sorry... I'm sorry, I can't... I can't do it!' She felt him let her go. 'I'm really sorry!' She was almost sobbing.

'No need to be. It's all right! I reneged on my promise to behave myself, didn't I?' he was smiling, recovering fast. 'I've always... You're so lovely, Anna!' He opened the door and went out.

When the sound of his car had died away she sat on the stairs and wept. Her legs were too weak to support her. She felt damp, and dishevelled and ashamed. She hadn't resisted at first. She had led him on, then cut him off. She was the worst kind of tease. Whatever did he think of her...? However could she face him? She was disgusted with herself!

CHAPTER FIVE

THE agency nurse, plump and dark-haired, not unlike Pam Fiske but a good thirty years younger, arrived with the 'earlies' shift, introducing herself to Anna as Ruth Bellingham.

'Anything that needs to be done, I'll do it,' she declared cheerfully, getting stuck in at once with bed-making, breakfasts and the distribution of mail. Barrier-nursing, she admitted, was new to her, but she was sure she could cope. She was looking forward to having her own special patient, and set about preparing and airing the side-ward long before Mrs Crowther was wheeled down the corridor at midday, her left leg in a trough.

Clive Stone, gowned and masked, went in to see her and view her X-ray films, which had come with her notes. Afterwards, leaving his gown on the back of the door, he went into the office where Anna was waiting in case he wanted to do a round. She was relieved that it was Clive and not Daniel. She dreaded seeing the latter. Thinking about it, and deciding how to play it had kept her awake half the night.

Clive proceeded to tell her that there was a short-stay patient coming up after lunch. 'Another trauma case—a sixty-year-old, who's fractured both her wrists. She's being reduced by Daniel under a general anaesthetic as we speak.'

'I've got two beds in the main ward.' Anna consulted the list. 'Mrs Pelly will be going into one of them, so this...' She looked at the notes. 'This Miss

Tebbit can go into the amputee's bed. She's being discharged this afternoon.'

'The sooner Crowther's swabs are taken and sent down to the labs, the better,' Clive emphasised in the officious manner he affected on the ward. 'Once she's cleared, *if* she's cleared, and if by then we've got a spare bed in the main ward, you'll have both sidewards free.'

Anna, who had already worked this out for herself, nodded in agreement. 'Ruth will take the swabs when Mrs Crowther has had her lunch and a rest.'

'Ruth being the new little chick who attended me in the side-ward.' Clive was signing half a dozen prescriptions Anna had ready for him.

'Yes, and she looks like being a find. I hope to have her next week as well.'

'She's probably booked if she's that good. I like the look of her. You know, Anna...' he clipped his pen to his pocket and leaned against the desk '...we're likely to be meeting socially in July at the event of the year.'

'I don't follow.' He had missed one prescription and she handed it back to him.

'Of course you do!' He signed the script. 'At Sir Guy's annual bash at his house in Grange Road. Remember last year—you can't have forgotten it!'

Anna's face cleared, 'No, I hadn't,' she said. 'I'd just simply not thought about it, but, yes, you're right, July is the month.'

'Be a bevy of top brass there, but we needn't tangle with them.' He slipped a hand over hers as it lay on the desk.

'I don't mean to tangle with anyone,' she said sharply, removing his hand.

'Of course not!' Laughing, Clive backed away to the

door, cannoning into Daniel who was trying to enter and treading on his toes.

'God, can't you look where you're going!' Daniel's face was thunderous.

'Sorry, sorry, and sorry again!' Totally unabashed, and clearly not in the least sorry, Clive took his leave.

'Bloody fool!' Daniel's face was contorted.

'It *was* an accident,' Anna said, for something to say. Daniel's appearance was making her shake.

After inspecting his feet as though expecting to see broken bones sticking out of his shoes, he began to tell her about the bilateral Colles' fracture.

'She's in Recovery at the moment. It sounds as though I'm making heavy weather about two simple reductions, but she was very shocked and in great pain when she was admitted. I'd like her in the ward for a couple of days until her pain subsides and she's had the chance of some physiotherapy. Her next of kin is a married sister living at Cletford Heath. Hopefully, she can go to her once she's discharged.'

'Has the sister been contacted?' Anna's head was well down over the notes.

'Yes, by A and E. No doubt she'll visit, probably this afternoon.'

There was a pause, a strained one. From way up the corridor Anna could hear the faint sound of the luncheon trolley being wheeled towards the ward doors. As its lumbering grey water-tank shape passed by the office, Daniel shut the door. 'I think,' he said, approaching the desk and sitting on its edge, 'that we've a little air to clear, haven't we, apropos last night?'

Her heart jerked. 'I didn't play fair!' she got in first.

'Not entirely, no.' His eyes met hers. 'But I should have had enough sense not to misread the signs, or place too much faith on them, especially when you'd just told me you're still holding a torch for Dudley. I'm older than you, and should be wiser, so let's shake on it, shall we, and just get on with our jobs?'

'That's what I'd like,' she told him with relief, a great weight rolling off her mind. And if she also felt, as they shook hands, a small pinprick of disappointment that he'd settled for friendship very easily, she refused to let it thrive. She was also determined to ignore the ache of longing she felt when their hands touched.

He asked her if Julie had got back all right, and Anna told him she had. 'She didn't turn a hair when I told her Mrs Court had been in our flat, except to say that I ought to make a life-size sketch of her, paste it on a board and put it on our landing, with the words "Get back down those stairs" printed bold and large.'

'I *like* it!' He laughed, stepping into the corridor. Things were back to normal again.

Mrs Pelly had been in the main ward for three days, and was clearly enjoying the company, when her daughter visited at the weekend. She stayed nearly an hour, too, which was unusual. Anna, who kept a vigilant eye on the ward when visitors were present, noticed that they were deep in conversation and that the old lady looked distressed, even more so when Doris had gone, so she went to investigate.

'Are you feeling a bit down, Mrs Pelly?' she asked, drawing the curtains round the bed for privacy. The old lady dabbed at her eyes and nodded. 'Can I help, do you think?'

'Doris and I have had a slight falling out, dear.' Mrs Pelly blew into a tissue. 'She thinks I should go into residential care, into a home, where I'll be properly looked after, she says. She wants to sell the house.'

'Oh, I see… Oh, dear!' Anna's mind raced. So that was what all the creeping about last Thursday had signified. 'What do *you* want?' she asked carefully, knowing she mustn't interfere.

'Go back to my proper home, back to Elvington Road. I've lived there since I was married. I went there as a bride. We had the whole house then, Harold and me. We planned a large family. In the end we only had Doris, but we both loved the house. I didn't have it converted until Harry died. The rent was very useful and I liked the company.'

'I expect Mrs Court will see things your way if you're really reluctant to sell,' Anna said, wary of upsetting her again now that her tears had stopped.

'The house belongs to Doris, dear. I made it over to her properly and legally ten years ago. It seemed right to do so. I mean, she is my daughter and her husband died when she was quite a young woman. Oh, she's going to sell. She saw Mr Brett, the agent, yesterday.'

'I didn't realise.' Anna felt flummoxed. So Doris Court was their landlady, which meant there was no hope for her and Julie.

'And that's another thing.' Mrs Pelly's plump hand fastened over her wrist. 'You and Miss Redman will have to find somewhere else to live. Doris said she'd see you about it… I'm ever so sorry, dear.'

'That's all right.' Anna squeezed the old lady's hand, but it didn't feel all right—it felt disturbing and somehow unpleasant. 'You mustn't worry about us,' she said. 'We'll miss you, though.'

'Oh, I won't be far.' For the first time her face creased in a smile. 'Doris has got me into Leahurst

Court, just off the Cletford Road. She thought it would be best for me to stay in the area where all my friends are. They can come and visit me so perhaps it won't be so bad after all. I'm old, Miss Chancellor, and I'll get even older. These things have to be faced.'

Going off duty at half past four, Anna's first thought was to rush home and tell Julie the news. Then she remembered that Julie and Sean were at the riding stables at Cletford Heath. They were both keen riders and had enough energy for six. The thought of sitting in the flat, contemplating its loss, didn't appeal. I'll go to the hotel, she decided, and tell my troubles to Dad. He'll be thrilled to hear I might be living there again, if only for a little while. At least…she quickened her pace across the courtyard…I have that option, but what about Julie? Where's she going to go?

Daniel's car was in the car park. On a Sunday that was unusual. He'd probably been called out to an accident case and was in Theatre. She found she wanted, very badly indeed, to tell him what had happened which was, after all, an extension of Thursday's run-in with Doris Court. Still, she couldn't very well hang about for him, could she? He might be ages. He might be dissecting someone's breastbone, or screwing and plating a leg. She wanted to see him, not solely because of the house, but just to see him, to talk to and be near him. If she was honest, she wanted his company.

When he hailed her from behind, and she spun round and saw him approaching from A and E, she felt a surge of relief and pleasure which she fervently hoped didn't show.

'What brings you here on the Sabbath?' she sang out, smiling at him.

'RTA on the motorway—a patient with a fractured skull, my turn on call. And your weekend on duty, I see. Going home now?' He looked his fill of her, his eyes taking in her tote bag hanging weightily from her shoulder, dragging the collar of her dress away from her creamy neck. 'I could give you a lift.' Her lashes were golden, lying like fans on her cheeks. 'But I'm sure you're going to tell me that your bike awaits in the sheds!'

'It does, but...' She hesitated, then heard herself say, 'If you can spare a minute, there's something...'

'We can talk in the car,' he said promptly. 'Nothing wrong, I hope? Look, on second thoughts, let's sit in the courtyard. The car'll be oven-hot.'

In the main courtyard, with its central fountain and slatted seats, she told him about the house dilemma and Mrs Pelly's distress. 'Oh, dear,' he said gravely, pursing up his mouth, 'so Mrs Court really was on a justifiable mission the other night. I have to say I'm not too surprised, except about the house ownership, of course.'

'Mrs Pelly is entirely in her hands!'

'She's put herself there, hasn't she? Still...' he slapped the knee of his jeans '...she'll have first-rate care at Leahurst Court—I've had good reports about it. All in all, Doris is probably doing the best long-term thing.'

'For herself maybe. She'll sell the house, bank the dosh, put her mother in the home, go back to Ipswich and forget all about her. And what about—?'

'It's their business.' Daniel gazed across the courtyard, narrowing his eyes against the sun and looking, Anna thought, as though he was bored with the whole thing, and probably with her. Even so, she couldn't

leave it, couldn't get up and go and let him do the
same. Damn it, he *should* listen!

'And what about us?' she demanded. 'What about
Julie and me? Where do we fit in? Well, we don't, do
we? We'll be out with the…the water, as soon as Doris
pulls the plug!'

Even that didn't seem to concern him, didn't make
him sit up and take notice. 'It may not happen for some
time, Anna.'

He was being patient, blow him. She seethed.

'I doubt if you'll get notice to quit until contracts
are exchanged, and that may be three or four months
along the line. A buyer's got to be found first.'

All this was said as though his thoughts were on
another plane. She could feel his distance, and her chagrin gave way to reason. For heaven's sake, there's no
earthly reason why he should concern himself with my
problems. He's been called out on a Sunday, which is
bad enough, without me bleating away, stopping him
from getting back home.

'Yes, well, I'll leave you to it,' she said, getting up
from the seat. He got up, too—he was never rude—but
sat down again almost at once.

'I'll sit here and sun myself for a bit. See you tomorrow,' he said, giving her hand a little jiggle, as
though switching her on to go.

It was the limit when she got home to find Doris
Court in the hall. 'I'd been hoping to see one or other
of you. Come in for a minute.' She indicated Mrs
Pelly's sitting-room, and then, once again, it all came
out… The sale of the house…already put in hand…the
fact that she was the owner. 'And Mother's going into
a home,' she concluded. 'Quite the best thing for her…

My mind will be at rest at last. I worry about her, you know.'

'I'm sure you do.' Anna's tongue was firmly in her cheek.

'I'm afraid, however…' and at last Doris got down to the nitty-gritty, '…that it will be necessary for you and your friend to move out—not immediately, but later when the sale is assured. Mr Brett has a key, and he'll be showing people round from time to time. They'll need to go into your flat, as well as down here.'

'I'll make sure there's nothing left lying around,' Anna said, as she went upstairs.

Julie was speechless when told the news that night. 'Hell!' she exploded. 'I didn't think it would come to this!'

Anna was grating cheese for a rarebit. 'Well, I suppose,' she said, 'it would have happened one day, considering Mrs Pelly's age.'

Julie snorted. 'She's got years of go in her yet, but what a softie to make the house over to Doris, putting her future in her hands!'

'She's her daughter. Mothers trust daughters.'

'Hell!' Julie said again, looking round the kitchen as though saying goodbye to it. 'Still…' She licked a flake of cheese off the end of her finger. 'There may be something wrong with the house that will put buyers off—like dry rot, or church beetle.'

'Black watch beetle, you clot!'

'Well, that, then!' They giggled together.

Anna put the rarebit under the grill, and with the evening taken up watching *Coronation Street*, then *Heartbeat*, followed by *London's Burning*, their precarious housing situation was put on hold.

*   *   *

Next day, being the first of Anna's three days off, she spat and polished the flat within an inch of its Victorian life. She reasoned that if people were coming round to view their part of the house, they would consider, with so much shine in evidence, that they must be excellent tenants and want to keep them on. You never know your luck, she told herself on Wednesday, coming back from the launderette, where the sitting-room curtains had shared a machine with their underclothes.

The phone in the hall was ringing as she let herself into the hall. Struggling with the laundry bag and lifting the receiver, she was astonished and startled to hear Daniel's deep, gravelly voice. Was there a crisis—a red alert? Had something happened on the ward?

'Anna,' his voice continued, 'Bretts have sent me particulars of the Elvington Road house. I got them yesterday.'

'Good *Lord*!' She heard her own gasp as she shut the front door with her foot. 'You mean, they think you might be interested?'

'I'm on their mailing list—they know I'm still looking. Why I'm ringing you is to tell you that Brett will be in touch—with you, I mean—to fix an appointment for me to view some time this evening. I thought I should warn you in case you got a shock!'

'I'm shocked now.'

'Sorry! Will about six be all right? I'll have James with me.'

'Fine, fine, couldn't be better. Julie will be home by then.' And I'll have time to iron the curtains and hang them up, she thought, hearing someone speak to him at the other end and the line go dead.

'Well, if he buys—*fantastic*!' That was Julie's comment when Anna told her the news. 'He won't turn us out. He'll like having us here. Anna, we'll be all *right*!'

'All living together, I *don't* think!' Anna exclaimed. 'I can't see him and his brother sardining it downstairs. They'll want the whole lot, upstairs and down, and that'll be the end of us.'

Even so, what Julie had said took root. Just supposing she was right and Daniel were to move in downstairs. How would she feel about him being there, with only a ceiling between them? She searched her mind and to her amazement discovered that the prospect of it appealed strongly. In short, she would love the idea.

They arrived—the anxious-to-please Mr Brett, Daniel, James and the languid Rowena—a few minutes after six. They toured downstairs first, taking their time. All the two girls could hear was the murmur of their voices, the opening and closing of doors, the tramp of their feet down the long passage to the kitchen, the yap of the dog next door. It was all Anna could do to stop Julie from lying face down on the landing, trying to glean every word.

They could see them when they went out into the back garden—the tall and dark Daniel, his bright-coloured brother and the bearded Mr Brett. There was no sign of Rowena but, judging from the sound of rushing water, she was trying the downstairs loo.

Anna's heart beat like a metronome when they came up the stairs. Everyone greeted everyone else, and Julie was introduced to Rowena and James. Mr Brett was bringing out his usual sales patter—close to the town centre, ideal for the hospital and the university, a much sought-after property.

There was more discussion downstairs, then more in the front garden. Anna was in the kitchen by then but

Julie, at her post by the living-room window, told her that Mr Brett was shaking hands with Daniel and going off, followed by James and that fair girl in a car with a roof rack on top.

'What about Daniel?' Anna's voice sounded weak.

'He's walking up the road...towards the river... He looks deep in thought.'

'You can't possibly tell his expression from this distance,' Anna snapped. She felt on tenterhooks. What had been decided, if anything had? She was literally panting to know.

When the sound of the doorbell reverberated through the house at seven o'clock she knew that it was Daniel, but it was Julie who flew down to answer it, Julie who brought him upstairs.

He entered the sitting-room, looking strained and anxious, and said, 'I like the house and James says he does, so I'm going to put in an offer.'

'I thought you might.' Anna forced a smile.

'You could probably tell I was interested when you mentioned on Sunday that Mrs Court was selling...'

'I noticed something. I noticed you seemed to go off into a dream!' This was less than polite and Anna knew it. She was just about to say something to put it right when Julie broke in.

'And I suppose this means you're going to throw us out?'

'Not throw out, no... Of course not!' Daniel's straight look encompassed them both.

'What, then?' Anna demanded in a nailing-down tone of voice.

'There's some wine left. I'll go and get it—it'll ease the atmosphere.' Julie sprang up and went into the kitchen, while Daniel and Anna measured glances, his as steely as hers.

'This isn't exactly easy for me,' he was saying when Julie came back, 'but if I don't buy, certainly someone else will.'

The wine, which Julie had brought back from Portugal after a holiday there last year, glugged into their glasses, and they started to drink. It tasted, to Anna, like vinegar, but at least it kept Julie quiet while Daniel explained what was going to happen once the house purchase went through. 'James will move in,' he said, 'into the downstairs part. You two, if you like, can stay where you are—at least for the present,' he added quickly as Julie made to erupt again. 'The lease on my Maitland House flat doesn't expire until Christmas. It makes sense for me to stay there until then, but afterwards—after Christmas—I shall move in here, when James and I will use it as a whole house, not as two flats.'

'It will make a very nice whole house,' Anna made herself say.

'We think so, yes, but I'm sorry it will make such an upheaval for you. Still, in seven months—and you needn't get out until I'm ready to move in—you should have found somewhere else to live.' He was looking only at Anna and not at Julie who was saying, so sensibly saying, that seven months was plenty of time to find somewhere else.

'As you say, we're bound to find something in that time, aren't we, Anna?'

'I suppose,' Anna said, trying to think in practical terms, 'that we'll be paying our rent, as usual, to Mrs Pelly, but after contracts are exchanged we'll pay you, as the new owner, until we move out.'

'That's about the size of it, yes.' Daniel was looking relieved. Anna wasn't. Blank-faced, she looked back at him. Unfairly, she felt that he was moving her and Julie about like puppets. He was getting what *he* wanted. Now, wasn't that just like a man? For one rash, dangerous moment she was tempted to say that they'd move out next week. Two things stopped her, however. The thought of Julie, for one, who would have nowhere to go, whereas she, Anna, had the hotel. The second thing was that she liked the house, liked living here, and wanted to do so for as long as she could—hang on by her bootstraps, in fact.

'Of course, you may get gazumped,' she heard herself say, and caught Julie's raised-eyebrow look. 'Or something else may happen.'

'You sound as though you hope it will,' Daniel said agreeably enough, but he got up to go without finishing his wine, nearly upsetting it as well.

Anna knew she should escort him downstairs, but she let Julie do it.

'You were a bit off, Annie, love,' Julie said when she returned. 'I know how you feel because I feel it, too, but we're lucky it's him who's buying. He's given us good notice and explained everything in detail, and I must say I liked his brother. *I* think it'll be rather fun to have someone young downstairs. I wonder if the anorexic-looking Rowena will be living here as well.'

Lying in bed that night and mulling the whole situation over, Anna realised only too well that she had been 'a bit off'. The person most deeply affected by it all was little Mrs Pelly.

It's her I should be thinking about. As for Julie and I, of course we'll find somewhere else to live. Daniel's fully entitled to buy the house. The thing is, of course, now that I know I'm never going to marry Rob I would like everything to revert to the way it was this time last year, with Mrs Pelly downstairs, as happy as Larry, and Julie and I up here. And that, Anna Chancellor, signifies that you're resistant to change which, in its turn, means that you're getting set in your ways—and *that's* a sign of old age!

That horrifying thought was followed by another just before she dropped off to sleep, which was that to-morrow she must seek out Daniel and apologise for her frosty attitude.

CHAPTER SIX

ANNA discovered there had been four new admissions during her three days at home—one of them a girl of her own age for elective surgery to her feet, a sixty-year-old for bone-grafting after an old fracture had failed to unite and two elderlies for cup arthroplasty. All had undergone surgery on Tuesday, so were two days post-op when she went into the ward to do her round and introduce herself.

There was to be a teaching round later—word had come through about it half an hour ago. Sir Guy and either Daniel or Clive, with half a dozen medics in tow, would be filing down the corridor at a little after ten. That meant it was kind to warn patients that they might be asked about themselves, and might also be asked to allow themselves to be examined, with the students looking on.

'But I want everyone in their beds,' Anna told them. 'Anyone who usually gets up can do so when the doctors have gone. Appointments down in Main Physio will have to wait as well.'

'Relax, Sister, we'll behave ourselves,' Kate Denver said. She was, Anna noticed, quite chirpy these days, becoming accustomed to her fixator and getting about in her wheelchair. Rumour had it that she was enjoying the company of a footballer in the day-room—a patient from Athelstone who'd had a meniscectomy and needed cheering up.

Mrs Crowther, her swabs being clear, was now in

the main ward beside Mrs Pelly, and Anna was pleased to see that the two were getting on. Mrs Pelly wanted Anna to stay and chat, but Anna told her she would later on. Then she hurried back to her office to start getting ready for the teaching round.

She asked Ruth Bellingham to help her, thankful that she'd still got her as part of the team. Together they got the notes out of the cabinet and into the truck for wheeling round, checking each set to make sure it was complete, with X-ray films attached, lab reports adhered to mount sheets and any change in medication filled in.

There were two panicky episodes—mislaying Mrs Ventnor's urine card and discovering that Haematology hadn't sent a report on Kate Denver's blood. All was well in the end, though. The card was on the ward desk, and Ruth's quick sprint down to the labs resulted in her returning with a handwritten note on Kate's red and white cell count.

'I could have done without this this morning,' Anna grumbled to Clive, who arrived with a set of notes which had gone to Records by mistake.

'Never mind, you'll have Dynamic Dan to support you.' He grinned unsympathetically. 'I've got a fracture clinic this morning, much to my relief.' Wanting to pinch Ruth Bellingham's bottom, but deciding he'd better not, he made his way back up the corridor *en route* for Outpatients Wing.

Ears pricked at the ready, Anna wasn't slow to hear the sound of the surgeons and half a dozen medics coming down from the landing doors. When their arrival at her door was imminent she went out to greet them, coming face to face with Sir Guy and Daniel who were standing abreast. Sir Guy was immaculate in his dark suit, and expressed the hope that she was well. Daniel, in his whiter-than-white long coat without a crease in sight, gathered together the hovering young medics, three of them female, then, with Anna pushing the truck at Sir Guy's heels, they all went into the ward.

There wasn't exactly a hush of expectancy from the patients, but they were all, apart from three who were dozing, watching the doors. It was a little like coming onto a stage set, Anna thought, as they first of all approached Mrs Barnes, supine on her plaster bed. Not unnaturally, she was of interest to the medics, who crowded round while Sir Guy explained about her spinal deformity and how it had been corrected. 'If you want to ask Mrs Barnes any questions about what it feels like to lie in a mould with only head and arms free, she may be good enough to tell you.'

Joan Barnes smiled. 'For washing I'm turned by two nurses, using a turning frame. I'm swung right over to face the floor, the shell is lifted off and I'm washed and powdered like a baby. The shell is wiped out, too, fitted back on me again and I'm turned to face the ceiling once more.'

'What about eating and drinking?' another medic asked.

'For drinks I have a flexible straw and a feeding cup. I can eat all right from a table thing that's swung across me. I was nervous at first, eating flat on my back. I used to think everything would drift sideways and come out of my ears!'

'You're my star patient,' Sir Guy told her, while over by the ward desk Daniel was telling part of the group that when X-rays confirmed that bony union had started Mrs Barnes would be lifted out of her mould and nursed on an ortho bed.

'Soon after that she'll have mobilising exercises, but she'll probably, as a precaution, go back into her shell at night. It's a long process...from admission to discharge she will most likely have been in here fourteen or sixteen weeks.'

In the aisle once more, they went on to Kate Denver's bed, where she displayed her steel-encased leg, not exactly with pride but with considerably less reluctance than she would have done six weeks ago.

'You're lucky to get to see this,' she said, smiling at the medics who were, after all, her own age. 'Next week it's due to come off, and I'll have a functional brace. I'll soon be walking again, or trying to, anyway.'

Once again Sir Guy trotted out his star patient accolade. But in actual fact she's Daniel's star, Ann thought, watching the latter's tactfulness in moving the group past the beds of two new patients who were trying to rest.

The round wore on...and on...and on. Would it never end? The mid-morning milky drinks trolley came in, but was shunted out by Ruth Bellingham. 'Not now—*wait!*' she snarled, alarming Rose Thrift, the domestic, whose first day on the job it was.

The two nurses seated at the ward desk were unnaturally quiet and there were none of the usual ward visits—no physiotherapist, no social worker, no phlebotomist, no anaesthetist tapping on chests. Even the phone ceased to ring, except out in the office where Jane Scott dealt with it.

Daniel and Sir Guy conferred together, sometimes changing a patient's medication or treatment, Anna jotting everything down. Her back ached from bending over the truck. Notes were pulled out and thrust back in. She couldn't worry about order—she'd sort everything in the office later. Oh, come on, Sir Guy, hurry *up*!

At last, at long last, it was all over. The medics were going off, and Anna, followed by Sir Guy and Daniel, repaired to the office, where there was more discussion on the two spinal patients, after which Sir Guy mentioned his annual party.

'You will both,' he said, 'be getting a formal invitation. It's on the second of July this year, so that's still four weeks to go. Charis and I are hoping for a warm evening so that we can turn some of you outside!'

Anna assured him she was looking forward to it, although right at that moment she was more concerned about the sheaf of admission forms Sir Guy was sitting on, which she had forgotten to clear from the chair.

Daniel was saying something similar and looking genuinely pleased. He had heard a little about this annual event from Clive who'd attended it the previous year.

'It'll be good to see you both there.' Sir Guy made a swift upward move, scattering papers in his wake, which he affected not to see. 'And now I must be off.' He moved to the door, which Daniel had open for him, 'I'm due at the Cletford General at two, and if I'm to get any lunch...' He looked back at Anna, then at Daniel as he passed him. 'I'll leave you in Anna's good hands,' he said, and went off up the corridor.

'Why does he think you want to be left here?' Anna was squatting down on her heels, retrieving her papers. Daniel bent down to help her.

'Could be,' he said, 'that he's a mind-reader as well as a bone-carpenter.' Before she could think up a suit-

able reply he went on to ask her if she really did intend
to go to the party.

'Why, yes.' She straightened up. 'I don't think it
would be good policy not to.'

'You mean, it's a royal command?'

'Something like that, but I went last year and it was
fantastic, it really was.' They were standing by the
desk, facing one another, and Daniel found himself
marvelling at the fine-grain pink and white of her skin,
at the way her mouth moved when she talked and
smiled, at the occasional glimpse of her tongue. He
shifted uncomfortably, stepping back a pace.

'Who actually goes?' he asked.

'All senior staff on our wing and one or two others,
like the SNO—out of courtesy—and consultants from
other hospitals where Sir Guy has beds. Nothing lower
than Sister rank from the nursing staff, then there's Dr
Smythe from the labs, the physio superintendent—all
those sort of bods. You'd be amazed at how many people there are when we all collect together. I was asked
last year as Acting Sister—I hadn't got the full post
then.' And I hadn't got Rob then, she thought. I hadn't
even *met* Rob then. I was fancy-free and I enjoyed
myself. Perhaps I will again.

Daniel was sitting on the arm of the chair that Sir
Guy had vacated a few minutes earlier. 'She has a
strange name—Sir Guy's wife,' he remarked conversationally.

'Charis—oh, she's half-Greek,' Anna said. 'She was
a staff nurse here at one time and he was the registrar,
like you are now. I wasn't here then, of course. I was
fifteen and still at school. But Sister Fiske told me
about them, said it was the romance of the year.'

'Interesting... Have they got any children?'

'Ten-year-old twins, both boys, and more recently, just a year ago, a baby girl.'

'A family man!' Daniel got to his feet.

'Very much so, yes.'

'Wouldn't suit me. I wouldn't want those tight ties.'

'I think,' Anna said, feeling her blood boil, 'you've made that particular point crystal-clear. You don't have to labour it—I'm not "after you" in any sense!'

'Hoity-toity, Sister Chancellor!' He folded his arms, and grinned. 'And may I say in turn that you have made *that* point clear before. There's no need to rub it in. I know a high fence when I see one! And now…' he made great play of looking at his watch '…I have to think of lunch. I'm relieving Clive in Clinic this afternoon, but I'll be up around three to see Kate's parents.' He reached the door and turned. 'Thanks for your help in the ward just now,' he said, all banter gone.

The trouble is, he's always so hyper-polite, Anna thought with a sigh when he'd gone, and I still haven't apologised to him, have I, for being so surly last night?

There was a spate of visitors that afternoon. Every bed had two people sitting alongside it. Flowers and fruit were piled up on the lockers, boxes of organic eggs were handed in to the ward kitchen—some people even brought tubs of ice cream which had to go into the fridge.

The whole ward, Anna thought, staring at it from her viewing window, looked like a market or camp, with some patients up and hobbling about on crutches, sticks or frames, some necessarily confined to bed with arms or legs in traction, the weights hanging down from their pulleys looking frighteningly vulnerable with so much traffic passing to and fro.

Mrs Barnes's teenage twins were sitting by her plaster bed. They were never particularly quiet, but their noise this afternoon was especially loud. Did they have to squeal with laughter like that? Why didn't their mother remind them that this was a hospital, not a circus? When a particularly loud yell made several other visitors turn and stare at them, Anna made her way into the ward, feeling anxious for her patients.

The twins, a boy and a girl, lapsed into quietness when they saw her approach, but she still felt it her duty to ask them to keep the noise down. 'There are one or two very ill patients in the ward—we have to consider them.' It was a quiet request, it couldn't have been more so, and Mrs Barnes backed Anna up.

'I've told them, Sister, a dozen times. They're just…they're just noisy kids.'

The 'kids', as she called them, were staring at Anna, the boy—a loutish youth—taking her in from top to toe, his jaw moving rhythmically as he champed on his chewing gum. They both burst out laughing as she walked away, and within minutes of her getting back to the office were as noisy as before.

'Either call Security and get them sent out, or leave it,' Jane Scott advised. 'If you go in again, they'll love it—that's what they're waiting for.'

'I'm not calling Security. Their mother would be mortified,' Anna said. There were times when Jane exceeded her authority, and this was one of them. But the disturbance continued, and when she looked once more through the wide viewing window and saw the boy was smoking, that clinched it once and for all. She went into the ward, not rushing but walking very determinedly past three beds, to face him. 'Will you put your cigarette out, please?' Her voice was low and controlled. 'Smoking, as I think you know, isn't allowed up here.'

'Who says?' A cloud of smoke was puffed into her face.

'Hospital rules, and *I* say so. Please, put it out.'

'Make me.' He came up close, the cigarette in his mouth. Anna stood her ground. She wouldn't move back or show that she was afraid. Behind her she could hear Mrs Barnes calling out to her son. Visitors were staring and the youth was so close he was almost on her feet. He gave her shoulder a shove, not hard, not hurting her, just a goading, inciting thrust. She was being made to look a fool, she should have sent for help. She could hardly see or breathe for smoke. It was pricking her eyes, making her choke. The boy's voice snarled, 'No one tells Derek Barnes what to do!'

Someone was coming down the ward from the end, approaching the boy from behind—a male someone, a male figure. Even through smarting eyes Anna knew, could sense, it was Daniel long before he had pinioned the boy's arms close to his sides and whispered into his ear, 'Now, I think you and I will take a little walk outside.'

And walk they did, or rather Daniel walked the boy, thrusting him in front of him and ignoring his cries which weren't very many as he'd been taken by surprise. The girl looked stricken as she ran beside them. Anna leaned against the wall for a steadying second before going over to Mrs Barnes.

'I'm so sorry, Sister... I'm so ashamed... Whatever must you think?' She was weeping, her tears flowing down her cheeks into her hair. Anna wiped them away, then sat down on the chair the boy had left, partly to spend a few minutes reassuring the poor woman but partly out of necessity. Her legs seemed to have turned to foam. It had been an unpleasant, nasty little incident, one that could have been avoided if she'd only done what Jane had advised and called Security.

'The lad wants a good leathering!' Mr Ventnor came up to say. From three beds along, sitting by his wife, he'd had a ringside seat, but his comment, probably a true one, upset Mrs Barnes even more. It was a good ten minutes before Anna could leave her and go back to the office, craving more than anything else a brief time on her own.

However, Daniel was in the office, a teatray in front of him with two cups already poured out. He handed one to her, saying nothing at all, except, 'Ah, there you are!' Then he watched her drink the tea, which he'd sweetened so much it made Anna gasp. She told him— she had to say something—that he'd arrived in the nick of time, exactly like a fictional hero, but no smile broke his face. 'Your staff nurse said you'd been having trouble since the start of visiting. Why didn't you call for help?'

Damn Jane, Anna thought, but said, looking at him very directly, 'Because I didn't want to. I didn't want to upset Mrs Barnes. I thought I could handle it without any kind of scene.'

'Instead of which,' Daniel said dryly, 'a worse scene was precipitated than the one you were hoping to prevent.'

'With hindsight, yes.' They were quarrelling…good! Anna felt like a good row. She'd had enough of this afternoon. Need he be quite so unkind? Need he be quite so unfair? 'So, what have you done with them— the troublemakers?' she asked. 'Where are they now?'

'Not on the premises, I made sure of that. I told them

that next time they were rude to you, or caused an upset on the ward, they'd be bounced out by experts, no holds barred. Have another cup of tea. I'll let you off the sugar this time,' he added more kindly, just as Jane tapped and entered, wanting to know how Anna was.

'Couldn't be better.' She meant well, Anna knew, but why couldn't she keep out?

'It was really unpleasant.' Jane was addressing Daniel. '*I* thought we should have sent for help, but Anna wasn't keen. Still, you arrived, Mr Mackay, and all was well in the end.'

'Sister did well.' Daniel's smile was for Anna. 'She would probably have coped without my intervention. I was just passing, as they say. And I mustn't forget the real purpose of my visit—to see Kate Denver's parents.'

'Do you want her notes?' Anna got up to get them, aware of a little glow in her chest region, doing far more good than the tea. The face she turned to him, as she gave him the notes, made him hold his breath.

'One thing gives me hope,' Daniel said, after Jane had gone out. 'You cast me in the role of hero just now, which simply can't be bad!'

He was gone before she could think up a suitably squashing reply—not that she wanted to quash him, quite the reverse. Watching him making his way down the ward to Kate Denver and her parents, looking at his long supple back as he bent to draw up a chair, she found herself thinking how much she liked him, thinking what fun he was. He could laugh at himself, moreover—something Rob could never have done. For the first time she touched on the possibility that she'd had a lucky escape.

*   *   *

Daniel waylaid her in the linen room next day to tell her that his offer for the Elvington Road house had been accepted by Mrs Court. 'I'm having a survey done on Tuesday,' he went on. 'Mrs Court is agreeable to James accompanying the surveyor, if that's all right with you and Julie.'

'Spot on,' Anna said. 'We'll both be at work so we won't be put out. There's a roof ladder in the garden shed—well, it's actually Julie's. She had a thing about being able to get into the loft in the event of the tank overflowing.'

'I'll remember that,' he said gravely, 'and I'll tell James.'

'And while I'm about it…' Anna stepped carefully over a bale of drawsheets '…I'd like to say that I'm glad you're buying the house. I didn't sound very glad the other night, I know… Sorry I was offhand.'

'I know you like living there.' His voice was soft, very nearly caressing. She had her back to him, locking the door, but she could feel him close behind, hear the jerk of his breathing, smell his maleness, and she knew she wanted him with a piercing, passionate fierceness that shook her to the core.

'Yes, well, these things happen,' she said, alluding to the house, at which he smiled and agreed, moving away in the direction of the corridor doors.

During the following week the house passed its structural survey, with only minor repairs to some roof battens needed and the repointing of a chimney stack.

'So, no dry rot to save our bacon,' Anna remarked to Julie. 'In a matter of weeks the house will belong to Daniel and he'll be our rightful landlord.'

'So he will,' Julie said absently. She was making white sauce at the stove.

'And I've been thinking.' Anna went to stand at her side. 'Don't you think it might be best for us to start looking for something else now, and not wait until nearly Christmas? I'd feel better about it somehow.'

Expecting a knowing and teasing comment from her friend, for Julie could scent what she called 'romance' in all male and female encounters, Anna was surprised when she removed the saucepan from the gas and suggested they sit down and talk.

'You sound very serious,' Anna said, following her into the sitting-room.

'I *am* serious. It *is* serious between Sean and me. Anna, he's got a job in Dublin on the *Irish Times*. He goes next month, he wants me to go, too…to live with him there.'

'Oh, *Julie!*'

'I've told him I will. I do love him, you know, and now, with all these changes here, it sort of all fits in.'

'But, Julie, *Ireland!*'

'It's Sean's homeland, and Dublin's his home town. There's a flat going, too, with the job, I mean. Oh, I really feel life's opening out for me, Anna. I hope you'll wish me luck.'

'Oh, Julie, of course I do.' She gave her friend a hug, 'I'm thrilled for you, I really am, and I think Sean's great!'

'Yes, he is, isn't he? Just great,' Julie enthused, feeling a sense of relief now that she'd told Anna her news. She'd been dreading doing so, bearing in mind the ill luck Anna had suffered. 'And it isn't as if,' she rattled on happily, 'I'll be landing you in the lurch. I mean, if

you don't want to look round for a smaller flat you
could always go back home.'

'True.' Yes, I'm easily disposed of, Anna added inside her head.

'And the hotel is near the hospital, so no problem
there.'

'True,' Anna repeated, struggling to make her genuinely glad feeling for Julie override the bleak one that
was creeping up on her.

She made tentative plans in bed that night, plans she
thought would work out. Julie would be leaving for
Ireland in four weeks' time, which is when *I'll* leave
this flat, she decided. The house transaction will probably be completed soon after that, so when James
moves in he can have the whole place to himself. I can
go back home, I know that, but I'd rather have my own
place so I'll answer one or two ads and look at the
hospital notice-board to see if any nursing staff are
looking for someone to share. I'll never find anyone as
compatible as Julie, or a flat I like as much as this
one—the whole house feels like a friend.

Towards the end of the week Mrs Pelly, now walking reasonably well with the aid of elbow crutches,
accosted her on her round and said how pleased she
was that the doctor was buying her house. 'Not that it
is mine, dear, but you know what I mean. You and
your friend will be able to stay there, won't you? I
mean, he wouldn't turn you out?'

Anxious to complete her round before the doctors
appeared, Anna didn't sit down but briefly explained
about Julie's and her future moves.

'Oh, dear, I never thought…' Mrs Pelly looked quite
upset. 'What a lot of changes are coming to pass just
because I was clumsy enough to fall and break my hip.

If that hadn't happened we could all have been living at the house for a few more years.' Until your daughter decided to cash it in, Anna thought but didn't say. There was no time to say any more, anyway, because Daniel was striding into the ward and down the centre aisle, singing out greetings to delighted patients on either side.

She went to meet him and they met at the central ward desk. 'Morning, Sister!'

'Mr Mackay.'

There was a twinkle in his eye, which Anna affected not to notice as she picked up the notes of the patients due for discharge, or 'signing off', as he called it, which was what he'd come for this morning.

They went first to Miss Iver, the bunion patient, who, at only six days post-op, was getting about well on crutches, although tending not to bear full weight on the whole of her foot, just steadying herself with the heel. As she had help at home Daniel decided to discharge her, emphasising that she would need to come in weekly for physiotherapy.

'Cut bones hurt, Miss Iver, but persevere, try to use the whole of your foot. Each day the pain will decrease.'

'I'll be glad to get home,' she said a little puffily, returning to the bedside on her sticks.

Mrs Crowther—the patient transferred from Cornwall—was told that she could go home after her flat had been inspected to make sure that her bed, lavatory and the chair she normally used were of a height that wouldn't put a strain on her leg.

'Supposing they're wrong—the wrong height?' She looked surprised and alarmed.

'Then adjustments will be made to get them right,'

Daniel explained. 'I'll get someone to go along today if you'll give Sister your key. In a few months' time, Mrs Crowther, none of this will apply. Your leg will be good and strong and you can sit at what height you like!'

'Well, thank goodness for that!' She laughed. 'And thank you for all you've done.'

'Which in your case isn't all that much. All the interesting part was done by the Duchy of Cornwall Infirmary!'

Daniel was in sparkling form this morning, Anna noticed, but, then, why shouldn't he be? He'd got everything going for him, hadn't he? Patients swooning at his feet, or very nearly. Why, even Mrs Ventnor, the Queen of Grumbling, was telling him how grateful she was. 'To be able to walk and lift my feet up, to be able to move without pain…without *any* pain. I'm free of it! It's like a miracle! And I can go home tomorrow, you say?'

Daniel was scribbling in her notes. 'Yes, tomorrow,' he said, handing the notes to Anna. 'You'll be given an Outpatients appointment for six weeks' time. Keep wearing your corset, by all means, till you feel confident without it. *And do walk each day*—exercise is good for you.'

'I'll remember.' She had a little weep, just to show how grateful she was, spotting the front of her green dressing-gown and blowing her nose.

With the round completed, Daniel stopped to talk to Mrs Pelly, who was crutch-walking back from the bathroom, concentrating hard. Anna, called to the phone, went to answer it in the office. It was Doris Court ringing to tell her that the Leahurst Nursing Home could take her mother on Saturday morning at eleven o'clock, once she'd been officially discharged.

'I think it's very probable that Mr Mackay will discharge her this morning,' Anna replied. Through the viewing window she could see the two of them sitting side by side, deep in conversation, Mrs Pelly's leg out on a rest. 'But I'll ring you back to confirm this later,' she added, 'so that you know what to tell Leahurst Court.'

'No need to do that,' Mrs Court said quickly. 'I'll leave you to tie up the ends—it's not easy for me from here. She'll be going by ambulance, I expect, so I needn't be there. I'll come down on Sunday, as usual. Perhaps you'll tell her that.'

'I'll tell her.' Anna was very nearly speechless.

'So don't ring me back unless there's some kind of hitch or hold-up.' She rang off, leaving Anna fuming at her attitude. Surely she realised that, for Mrs Pelly, going into a nursing home on a permanent basis was a traumatic event. She needed to have someone of her own with her, and what about all the little bits and pieces she'd want to take from Elvington Road? 'Oh, that woman really does get my goat,' she was saying under her breath as Daniel put his head round the door.

'I've just discharged Mrs Pelly,' he informed her. 'So, where does she go from here?'

'To the nursing home, on Saturday.' Anna told him about Mrs Court's call. 'I'm to make all the arrangements, which I don't actually mind, but you'd think Doris would want to do it. I feel so sorry for the poor old lady.'

'She'll have first-class care at Leahurst,' Daniel said, watching Anna as she turned to the cabinet to get Mrs Pelly's notes out.

'Yes, I know. You said that before.' She handed him the folder. 'But I dare say it's not exactly the way she wanted to end up.'

He wrote in the notes, bending over the desk, while Anna stood at the window, looking down into the yard at the ambulance station over to the right, at the van turning in at the gates, at the blaze of multicoloured wallflowers in the garden of the medical school. She sighed and he heard her.

'Why the heavy breathing?' He was clipping his pen to his coat.

'Oh, this and that...life in general!' She tried to laugh it off.

'Mrs Pelly's just told me that you and your friend are leaving Elvington Road this month. Is that true or has she got confused?' He looked at her under his brows, his chin tucked into his chest.

'It's true enough,' Anna said.

'May I ask why...why the rush?'

'Because Julie's going to Ireland with her boyfriend, who has a job out there. I shall have to get out anyway at Christmas, so I may as well make the move now.'

'So I'm never to be your landlord, not even for a few months?' He was teasing her, or she thought he was.

'Sadly, no.' She laughed.

He started to say something else, but her phone rang again, and as her hand went to it she heard him say as he turned to the door, 'Look, I'd like to talk about it. Meet me in the shop when you come off duty. I'll be in the garden out at the back. I'll wait there till you come.'

She wanted to tell him that there was nothing to talk

MILLS & BOON®

An Important Message from The Editors of Mills & Boon®

Dear Reader,

Because you've chosen to read one of our romance novels, we'd like to say "thank you"!

And, as a **special way** to thank you, we've selected <u>four more</u> of the <u>books</u> you love so much **and** a welcome gift to send you absolutely <u>FREE!</u>

Please enjoy them with our compliments...

Tessa Shapcott

Editor, Mills & Boon

P.S. And because we value our customers we've attached something extra inside...

PEEL OFF AND PLACE INSIDE

How to validate your Editor's Free Gift "Thank You"

1. **Peel off the Free Gift Seal** from the front cover. Place it in the space provided to the right. This automatically entitles you to receive four free books and a beautiful goldtone Austrian crystal necklace.

2. **Complete your details** on the card, detach along the dotted line, and post it back to us. No stamp needed. We'll then send you four free novels from the Medical Romance™ series. These books have a retail value of £2.40, but are yours to keep absolutely free.

3. **Enjoy the read.** We hope that after receiving your free books you'll want to remain a subscriber. But the choice is yours - to continue or cancel, any time at all! So why not accept our no risk invitation? You'll be glad you did.

Your satisfaction is guaranteed

You're under no obligation to buy anything. We charge you nothing for your introductory parcel. And you don't have to make any minimum number of purchases – not even one! Thousands of readers have already discovered that the Reader Service is the most convenient way of enjoying the latest new romance novels before they are available in the shops. Of course, postage and packing is completely FREE.

Tessa Shapcott

Editor, Mills & Boon

about, she had made up her mind, but she had to answer the phone and, anyway, he was giving her no chance for he was moving off up the corridor at his usual rate.

CHAPTER SEVEN

THE hospital shop, which sold newspapers, flowers and confectionery, had a small tea and coffee bar, and a square of walled garden abutting the medical school at the back.

Daniel was already there, Anna saw, as she pushed her way through the shop, which was always crowded at off-duty times, with staff buying papers or snatching a cuppa before going home. The garden took the over-spill, but this evening it was all but deserted as Anna joined Daniel on one of the seats.

'Good, you've come.' He laid his paper on the seat. 'I thought you might forget.'

'I very much doubt if you thought any such thing!' Anna laughed, secure in the knowledge that in her off-duty state they could talk on a level and not as doctor and nurse. 'Why, though, did you want me here? Is it about the flat?'

'Of course.' He turned round to face her. 'I mean, why the exodus?'

'I told you why. Julie's going, and as I'll have to eventually, I thought it may as well be now. With only six months to go, it's hardly worthwhile casting around for someone to share.'

'Is it a question of rent, because once the house is mine—?'

'It's nothing to do with rent,' she said a little over-emphatically. 'I like the house, I've loved being there, but it's moving time all round!'

'You don't have to go, not even at Christmas,' he said quietly. 'With Julie gone there'll be loads of room for the three of us—James, you and I.'

'It'd be a very strange household.' She was trying to steady her voice.

'Not for these days, surely,' Daniel said coolly. 'Mixed sharing is hardly new. There's no hidden agenda, Anna. I'm not plotting to share your bed. All it would mean would be a little rearrangement of the living accommodation.'

'I don't think it would work,' she managed to say, for she knew that it wouldn't. She would never be at rest, never be at ease—not with him so close. And he would know that, sense it, and they *would* end up in bed... And she couldn't stand being dumped by him, which would happen in the end. So, self-preservation was well to the fore as she added for good measure, 'In any case, I feel that my parents would like me home for a bit.'

'Well, in that case no argument,' he said, snappishly for him. There was a flash in his eye that could have been anger, and the skin round his jaw was tight. She was surprised and upset, as the last thing she wanted was to be at odds with him.

'Perhaps we should go,' she said unhappily, noting that the little garden was fast emptying as staff went off to their homes and rooms.

'In a minute. There's one thing more.' He was staring straight ahead. 'I'm going with Mrs Pelly to Leahurst Court on Saturday morning, just to see her in. I wondered if you, as her erstwhile lodger, would like to come as well—perhaps ride in the ambulance with her while I follow by car. That is, of course, if you're off duty, and have an hour to spare.'

Thank goodness, she thought, this bit is easy, and because it was she smiled, making him look away for a different reason now, while she told him, a little breathlessly, 'Daniel, I was going, anyway. I've already told Mrs Pelly I would, so, yes, we can both go, make an occasion of it for her! I think it's a brilliant idea!'

'So I've found favour at last, have I?' He was looking at her again, and she at him. They were so close she could see the tawny flecks in his eyes. She could see the hard slant of his cheek-bones, the powerful masculine nose…his mouth firm and evenly-lipped moving nearer to hers. She didn't move, couldn't move, didn't want to move. When he kissed her it was quick…and light…and sweet…and she was totally disarmed and pliant, enchanted beyond belief. She had never, not even at their steamiest moments, felt like this with Rob.

'What was that for?' she managed to joke.

'For agreeing with me for once!' He stroked her nose and her chin with gentle fingers. He had beautiful surgeon's hands, lover's hands, too, and she yearned for their touch. Then, suddenly aware of where they were, she got to her feet, talking about getting home before it started to rain.

It looked like rain—ominous clouds were banking up from the west. Daniel, beside her now, was buttoning his jacket up. 'I shan't see you tomorrow,' he told her as they walked back through the shop and out into the main yard towards the parking lot. 'Sir Guy and I are operating out at Cletford Heath, so about Saturday…' They halted at his car. 'I'll pick you up from Elvington Road at about ten forty-five. Does that suit?' The car door was open and he prepared to get inside.

'Well, yes, it suits me perfectly, but I *could* come on my bike.'

'I thought you'd say that.' Sitting in the car now, he smiled up at her. 'I'm beginning to dislike that bike of yours, Sister Chancellor, and I don't want to so much as set eyes on it on Saturday, so keep it hidden away!'

'Yes, Mr Mackay, whatever you say!'

'Now, that,' he said, before he drove away, 'is very dangerous talk.'

It wasn't, Anna thought as she cycled home, just the talk that was dangerous. Their relationship—if one could call it that—had changed from that of a few weeks ago. It had sharpened up, become piercing, intense, and she couldn't *believe* this had happened. Why, she was only just getting over Rob, wasn't she? Admitting that, even realising that, shook her to the core.

I don't love Daniel, it's just explosive sex, and nothing in this world would draw me into an affair with anyone I didn't truly love…or who didn't love me, she added silently.

It rained incessantly all day Friday, and it was still pelting down when the green BMW turned into Elvington Road on Saturday morning.

'He's here!' Julie called out to Anna from her position by the sitting-room window. 'He's getting out and coming to the door under a golfing umbrella. He doesn't intend you to get wet!'

'I'm not likely to, am I?' Anna appeared in a scarlet crinkle mack and matching hat, her hair in a single plait lying over one shoulder.

'See you later, and don't forget you promised to come tonight.' Julie was referring to the fair on Heaver Common, which came to the town every June. She and

Sean were going and they wanted her with them, or at least they said they did. Meanwhile, as the chiming of the doorbell pealed through the house she hurried down the stairs.

'Off we go... Best foot forward!' That was Daniel's informal greeting, and down the wet brick path they sprinted out to the waiting car. 'Not the best of mornings, I'm afraid!'

He drove to the top of the road to turn, then whooshed back down it, Julie waving from the window as they passed.

'Good of you to give up your Saturday morning,' he remarked, just a shade stiffly, Anna thought. He looked stiff, too, rigid about his shoulders and neck.

'I could say the same about you,' she retorted, facing the front again, looking through the wide area of windscreen cleared by the wipers whose to-and-fro action and rhythmic clicking made her feel hypnotised.

'Oh, well, all in a good cause.' He swung the wheel to the left, driving slowly towards the roundabout and the start of Princes Parade, devoid of bicycling students now that the long vac had begun.

'How's James?' Anna asked, for something to say.

'Oh, going to take part in some kind of boat race up beyond Claysbite Lock. I've promised to cheer him on from the bank, although, if this downpour keeps on, they'll cancel, I should think.'

'The boat crews go out in any weather. There are always enough local students to make up the numbers, even during vacations.'

'James being one of them. But he'll be up in Scotland soon, if our parents have anything to do with it. Now, Anna, here we are,' he said a little more warmly as they drove onto the hospital precinct. He backed the car under the canopy, and Anna got out in the dry, leaving him there, looking out at her as she rustled in her red mack through the automatic doors.

Going swiftly up to the ortho floor, she found the ambulance crew—a friendly woman and a man—getting Mrs Pelly stretchered up. Jane, supremely in charge, informed Anna that the old lady's leg was going in a trough. 'No sense in taking chances!'

'Oh, quite!' Anna said.

'I could walk on my sticks,' Mrs Pelly protested, but her relief when Anna appeared was plain to see, and she held the younger woman's hand all the way down the corridor to the lifts.

The ambulance was waiting just in front of Daniel's car, and he himself was coming forward to greet Mrs Pelly and hand her a bunch of mixed flowers which he'd got from the hospital shop.

'So kind of him,' Mrs Pelly said in the ambulance, holding the flowers to her chest. She was very moved, on the edge of tears, which surprised Anna not at all. She was losing her independent life and going into the care of strangers, not just for a few prescribed weeks but until the end of her natural life. It was best, Anna thought, not to say too much, and their talk on the ten-minute journey was kept to safe subjects like the comfort of the newly equipped ambulance and the rain beating down on its roof.

Matron Brabazon, a large lady with an even larger voice, was in the hall of Leahurst Court to welcome Mrs Pelly and to shake hands with Anna and Daniel. 'How lovely of you to come along... Now, when we've got Mrs Pelly settled in you must let me show you around!'

Anna, a good twenty yards ahead, following the

stretcher down a seemingly endless corridor, could hear every word she said. Her voice literally bounced off the walls—very nearly echoed, in fact.

Mrs Pelly's room was on the ground floor and looked out onto the grounds. It was spotlessly clean and adequately furnished. 'I like the curtains,' she said, fingering them carefully to see if they were lined. The bed had a duvet of the same material. 'Now, this is *your room*, Mrs Pelly,' Matron emphasised. 'If you want to have your meals in here, you can. If you want company there's the dining-room a little way down the passage. You've a washbasin in here, as you can see, and the bathroom is next door.'

Anna marked—and liked—the way she spoke directly to the old lady, giving her the whole of her attention, not looking round at Daniel and her for an appreciative audience. 'I shall come and see you every morning when I do my round, and you'll be meeting the other nurses, one by one. I'll leave you now to chat with your friends!' A buck-toothed smile accompanied this last remark before she swept to the door, saying that she'd return to show them round in about half an hour.

'So, what do you think of it?' Daniel smiled over at Mrs Pelly in her chair. She looked a little flushed and a strand of hair had broken loose from its bun, but on the whole, Anna thought, standing beside her, not too bad.

'I'll have a lovely view when it's not raining.' She moved her leg with care. 'Its quite nice, better than I thought, and when Doris brings my clothes tomorrow, and one or two other things from the house, I'll like it even more. Why don't you sit on the bed, dear?' She craned her neck back to Anna. Daniel, tall in light trousers and dark blazer, was investigating the room—the wardrobe, the chest of drawers, the pictures on the walls. The bed was a hospital type on wheels. There was a gadget for altering its height, a strip light over its head, a bell-push within reach.

Shortly before the half-hour was up a young nurse came to take Mrs Pelly for a walk down the corridor. She brought a wheelchair, but agreed at once when the old lady wanted to walk. Behind her loomed and ballooned the vast figure of Matron, arriving to take Daniel and Anna on their tour.

'I hadn't bargained for this,' Daniel said into Anna's ear as they mounted the stairs.

'Me neither!' She stifled a giggle.

'We could take the lift, but I seldom do,' Matron was informing them. 'The patients are the ones who need it. We able bodies should walk.' Her walking, Anna noticed, was more like rock-climbing, giving the impression that she was secretly itching to take the stairs three at a time.

Once on the first landing they were shown the nursing wing, where everything was relatively quiet—most of the patients sitting quietly in their rooms like Mrs Pelly downstairs. On the other side of the building, however, in the residential care section, all was buzzing life. The corridors were crowded with older people, manoeuvring themselves along on sticks, or Zimmers, or walking frames, some being helped by nurses.

'They're making for the dining-room,' Matron explained. 'We start serving lunch at twelve.'

Noting that they were back on the ground floor and near the corridor where they'd come in, Daniel suggested to Anna that she should say goodbye to Mrs

Pelly, after which they could be on their way. 'I'll wait here for you,' he said.

Turning to Matron, he was just about to thank her for her tour when a clap of thunder, like a bomb going off, made all three of them flinch.

'Must be right overhead,' Matron mouthed, and even as she spoke a flash of lightning scissored the air, making the television they could see through in the lounge hiss like a nestful of snakes. It was the start of the storm, not the end, and it continued to rage.

'There's no question of you leaving in this,' Matron shrieked, comforting alarmed residents. 'Such a nuisance, coming now, just as they're about to eat! As for you, Mr Mackay, you and Sister must lunch here. We have a guest room where we occasionally serve meals for visitors—it's just round the corner here. I'll get Kirsty to lay the table and serve you as soon as she can. It'll be cold fare, but nutritious—everything organic and home-grown, nothing Frankenstein-raised!'

All this was conveyed in a shout as the storm crashed and battered away, while the lightning caused the electric lights, which had had to be switched on, to flicker. 'It's true. I can't drive in this,' Daniel mouthed at Anna, who was tugging at his sleeve, trying to get him to refuse the lunch invitation.

'Tell her we'll wait in the hall,' she insisted, but he either didn't hear or elected not to do so for he was nodding at Matron, plainly going through the motions of accepting her offer, his lips forming the words 'very kind'. There was nothing for it but to give in gracefully, and say 'very kind' herself.

They were shown into the room by the maid who'd be bringing their food. Leaving Daniel to look round— he was a dab hand at inspecting rooms—Anna found her way back to Mrs Pelly, who was eating plaice and green beans.

'We're just going,' she said, which was a small lie, of course, 'but I'll be back to visit you every week, and that's a promise, cross my heart!' She was relieved to see that the old lady was enjoying her lunch. She even made a joke about the storm. 'It's God's way of getting my new life off with a bang,' she said.

When Anna got back to the little dining-room, there was a white cloth on the table, a bowl of salad, another of potatoes and a dish of mixed cold meats. 'As I said before…' Daniel pulled out a chair for her '…this isn't quite what I planned.'

'We could have waited in the hall easily enough. Storms don't last for ever.'

'Whereas this one made its appearance at exactly the right time.' He was helping himself to new potatoes, looking down at his plate.

'Whatever do you mean?' Anna demanded, although inside she was feeling a little differently…quite pleased to be where she was.

'I mean…' Daniel beamed at her across the table '…we're having lunch together, aren't we, in pleasant surroundings?' He waved at the garden outside. 'Whereas if I'd asked you to a restaurant in the town you'd have turned me down flat.'

'I don't know about flat…' a wedge of tomato eluded Anna's fork '…but I couldn't have come. I'm supposed to be eating at the hotel. My grandparents, from Norfolk, are down here for the day.'

'Good Lord.' Daniel looked stricken. 'Why ever didn't you say? I'd have got you there somehow—eye of the storm or not.'

'As you were busy pretty-speeching Matron,' Anna

said, 'I didn't like to spoil things, did I? Anyway, it's all sorted. When I went along to see Mrs Pelly I discovered a pay-phone, so I rang up and explained the situation to my mother—not that she liked it much.'

'We'll make swift tracks just as soon as we've finished.'

'Yes, even the rain has stopped now.' Anna broke off as Kirsty came in with a steaming dish of apple Charlotte and a small jug of cream.

'Matron said to tell you…' she gave them each a plate '…that the apples are home-grown, too.'

'How about the cream—got your own cow?' Daniel joked.

He was taken seriously, however, and told, 'No, the cream came from Unigate.'

'There you are, you see, you shouldn't tease young girls,' Anna said when she'd gone. She served out the Charlotte evenly. She was hungry, she found. If Daniel wanted more that was just too bad. 'So,' she remarked, trying not to crunch too audibly, 'looks like you'll be able to be cheer-man by the river this afternoon, after all.'

'Afraid so,' he sighed.

Anna sighed too. 'I've been roped into going to the fair with Julie and Sean tonight.'

'Likewise myself with James and Rowena.'

'Oh, really?'

A small silence fell, broken by Daniel. 'Perhaps we could all meet there—might be fun.'

'What time are you going?'

'About half past nine. It's much the best when it's all lit up, more…exciting.' His eyes took her in as she sat there in her sleeveless green dress, looking thoughtfully back at him.

'That's when we're starting off, roughly speaking,' she said. 'I shan't be back from the hotel much before then.'

'Then let's meet…arrange it…form a sixsome…'

'Sextet,' she corrected unthinkingly, then blushed scarlet under his gaze.

'Quite,' he said, laying his hand over hers on the table top. She let it stay there—a warm weld, affecting far more than her hand. 'Adorable Anna, so cautious of me, of every move I make. I would never do anything to harm you, surely you realise that. I'd never seduce you into a situation which in your heart you didn't want.'

'My heart and head talk different languages,' she admitted in shaky tones just as Matron plunged in, and, had she known it, plunged her visitors back to earth.

'The storm is over,' she announced dramatically, 'but would you like to stay for coffee?'

They didn't and said so politely. Anna put her mack back on, which covered her up from neck to knee. They were escorted to the front door by Matron, Daniel slipping her a note to put in her Age Concern box.

'Good of you to do that,' Anna said when they were in the car. 'There's no reason why Leahurst Court should provide us with food.'

'Particularly when it's *all organic*!' Daniel mimicked Matron's voice, making Anna laugh and her spirits rise as they drove down the hill in the warm, bright sunshine which was making the road steam.

'You'll need your waders for Claysbite,' she cautioned. 'The river swells high there before it runs into the fens.'

'The only rubbers I possess are my theatre boots, but I'll suffer in a good cause. Sometimes I wish my young brother wasn't so keen on watersports,' Daniel said resignedly, jerking his sun-flap down. 'Now, Anna,' he continued as they drove down Silver Street, 'we've got to arrange about tonight, exactly where we are meeting. According to James, the fair is enormous and we don't want to leave it to chance. Being a Saturday—the best night of the week—it's bound to be crowded out.'

Anna felt a thrill of excitement at the prospect. 'Oh, let's meet by the dodgems,' she said. 'There are bound to be dodgems. Let's meet there between half past nine and ten. *I'll* be there, even if Sean and Julie have sloped off.'

'Agreed!'

Daniel's hand left the wheel for a second as he turned into the hotel drive, just as the figure of a woman streaked in front of the car, all but under his wheels. He braked violently. 'Bloody hell!' he shouted, getting out. 'Couldn't you see me coming?' Shaken, he couldn't believe he hadn't hit her. 'This is a cars-only drive!'

'I know that, I own it.' Lois Chancellor looked coolly back at him. By this time Anna was out of the car.

'Mummy, this is Daniel…Daniel Mackay. Daniel, this is my mother.'

'Oh, dear!' he put out his hand, which she took. 'Sorry I swore at you.'

'You didn't swear *at* me, you simply swore.' Her cool look was still apparent. 'This route is a short cut to our private apartments, and I was rushing to get back. I'm glad you didn't run over me…on the day my parents are here!' When she smiled it was Anna's smile all over again, and Daniel responded to it at once.

'You can turn here,' Anna said. 'We can walk the

rest of the way.' Slipping her arm in her mother's, she backed away from the car.

'OK, if you're sure… See you at the fair!' He slipped behind the wheel. 'Nice to meet you, Mrs Chancellor.'

'You must come again,' she said. They both waved as he reversed round the drive entrance, and went off down the road.

'Great car, attractive man,' Lois observed. 'How is it that medical bods are always endowed with good looks? And what's all this about going to the fair—romance on the swings?'

'Six of us are going—it's not a twosome! Meanwhile, I'm here to see Granny and Grandad,' Anna said, trying to change the subject by mentioning the storm and sticking to it till they got inside the hotel.

CHAPTER EIGHT

THEY travelled to the fair in Sean's Ford Escort, starting out from Elvington Road at a little before half past nine. They were all geared up for it, both in dress and anticipation—Anna in cream jeans and sweater, Sean and Julie in identical track suits of blue and white.

Long before they got to the common they could see the glow in the sky, hear the pulsating throb of music, see the traffic thickening up. Coaches and charabancs slowed cars to a crawl. 'It's worse than a bank holiday,' Sean grumbled good-humouredly, stuck behind a bus.

'Great, though, isn't it?' Anna hugged herself in the back seat. It was going to be a fun night; excitement ran in her veins. She couldn't remember the last time she'd felt so carefree and light.

Ten minutes more of stop-and-start, another five to park the car, then they were passing through the north side entrance into the glittering heart of the annual fair that drew crowds from far and wide.

Daniel was waiting by the dodgems. Anna spotted him instantly—top-heavy in an Arran sweater, narrow-hipped in blue jeans. Her insides stirred at the sight of him. As though pulled by a tugging cord, she went to stand at his side, while Julie introduced Sean.

'James and Rowena are already "dodging". There they are—look!' Daniel pointed out James who was manoeuvring rapidly, Rowena beside him, her arms well inside the hurtling red car, her fair hair looking white. When the cars ground to a halt, and Sean had once more been introduced, all six toured the side-shows, James winning a Felix cat at the shooting range, Anna a glove puppet at hoop-la, Daniel excelling at the coconut shy but refusing to take the three hairy nuts he won.

'I'm damned if I'm going to cart those around with me all evening,' he said. 'I don't even like the things!'

The rides came next and they went on them all, Sean complaining that there was no Big Terror Ride any-where in sight.

'It's an old-fashioned, old-type fair, not a theme park,' Daniel said. 'Tonight I feel this takes some beating. Now, how about another go on the roundabout? I so much want to see Anna astride one of those pea-cocks!'

He pushed the back of her head gently with the flat of his hand, and she laughed up at him as they hurried to take their places in the queue for the big steam-driven roundabout, currently belching out 'The Anniversary Waltz' from its hot, hissing centre, changing to 'Love and Marriage' as the six of them mounted their steeds.

Anna selected her peacock, Daniel the horse at her side, and off they went, slowly at first, then faster and faster, Anna's hair flew back in a golden plume, her skin-tight jeans stretched to full capacity—that peacock had a broad back. She wasn't too sorry when at the end of the ride Daniel lifted her down.

Refreshments were suggested by him, but the others wanted to dance. There was a disco in a marquee on the south side of the ground. 'Well, I'm for Daniel's suggestion. I'm parched *and* I'm hungry.' Anna, still feeling a whirling sensation from the roundabout, was leaning against Daniel's side.

'OK, well, let's split up,' Sean suggested. 'When you two have done stuffing yourselves come along to the disco. It'll be open for another hour at least.'

'Yes, we'll see you there.' Julie flipped a kiss at them both, but then, just to hold things up, Rowena had another idea.

'Let's have our fortunes told first—look, just over there in that caravan thing. The teller is a proper Romany, it says so at the door.'

Anna was dubious, Julie ecstatic and the three males shook their heads but agreed that the girls should venture in while they waited outside.

Julie was the guinea-pig, going in first. When she came out she looked bemused. 'She read my palm first, then peered into her ball, muttering to herself. She looked more like a witch than a gypsy, but perhaps she's both.'

'You haven't told us what she said yet,' James prompted. Julie was looking at Sean.

'She said I was on the threshhold of much change in my life... Said I was going across the sea...'

'That'd be the Irish sea!' Sean was grinning broadly now.

'She also said I'd have five children—three boys and two girls!'

'When?' Sean pretended to be winded.

'She didn't specify when, except to say that I would live to a very great age and have good health most of the time. I don't know whether to believe her or not, but she got the sea bit right. Let's sit down while we wait for Rowena, shall we?' She jerked Sean down onto the grass.

Rowena looked upset when she emerged, and didn't, Anna thought, seem to want to talk about what she'd been told. 'Oh, come on, Rowena, you can't keep it to yourself,' James cajoled.

'She said,' Rowena began haltingly, 'that I was going out to the Orient, and that shook me, it really did. I mean, I'm going next week. She also said I must try to persuade the one I love to come with me. If I didn't, if I left him behind, I'd regret it.' She held James's eyes steadily. 'I think she was trying to say that, left here in England, you'd take up with someone else.'

'Oh, rubbish,' James exploded. 'The woman's a nutter! Don't think any more about it, poppet!' But Anna saw the little shudder Rowena gave before he put his arms round her.

'Well, I'm not going in and that's flat!' she announced dramatically.

'Chicken!' Sean teased.

'Call it what you like!'

'If Anna doesn't want to, she doesn't have to,' Daniel said quietly. 'Now, why don't you four go and dance, and leave us to our own ploys?'

'Wowee!' James exploded.

Julie tugged Sean up from the grass. 'See you in half an hour,' they chorused. 'We'll stay at the disco till you come!'

Daniel held out his hand to Anna and she slipped hers into it, glad of its comforting warmth. All that talk of fortune-telling had somehow chilled her blood.

'Rowena was really upset, Daniel,' she said as they waited at one of the awninged refreshment stalls for ham rolls and coffee and, with luck, fruit and ice cream.

'Yes, I think she was. Of course, James *does* play the field a bit. She knows that. For all her fragile looks, Rowena's sensible, with a brain.'

'Let me take some of that.' They were being served. Rolls, cheese and crackers and celery sticks were being packed for them in two boxes. Then, in plastic pots with little lids, came strawberries and ice cream.

'I've got a flask of coffee in the car—one of James's better ideas—so if we make our way over in that direction, not far from the First-Aid vans, we can sit down in peace, in the car or out, whichever you please.'

They set off with their spoils, Daniel leading the way through the noisy, jostling crowd, past the side-stalls with their naphtha flares, past the puppet theatre, the helter-skelter, the flying boat swings, to the oasis of space by the First-Aid Post, where the car park began, and James's old Metro stood. 'I had no intention,' Daniel said, unlocking its door, 'of chancing the BMW on Heaver Common tonight!'

'I don't blame you!'

'I drove here, though, to give James and Rowena quality time in the back. After all, she does fly off on Monday and won't be back for three months.'

'She's really worried about leaving James.'

'Yes, I know. She was worried even before that so-and-so fortune-teller made things worse.'

'She was right about some things—the fortune-teller, I mean.' Anna took a groundsheet from Daniel and spread it on the ground. 'That's why I wouldn't go in myself, just in case she *was* genuine. I don't want to know what's going to happen to me and be frightened half to death!'

'Romanies are supposed to have what we in Scotland call "the sight". Ah, good.' His voice sounded muffled from inside the car. 'I've found the coffee. Now we can get started. You're sure you want to sit outside?'

'Oh, yes, please, let's. It's quite warm and we can

look on from afar. I just hope no one's stretchered here with a broken limb and you have to do your stuff!'

'Don't even think about it! I'm strictly speaking *off* call. Tonight I'm just plain Daniel Mackay with no letters after my name.'

'Shame on you!'

'Eat up, woman, and stop berating me!' He kissed her cheek as she leaned over to open one of the cartons. 'You look,' he said, 'like a golden-tressed mermaid, with your hair hanging loose like that.'

'It gets in the way. I should tie it back.' But she was glad of its screening curtain as she bent her head to eat. Her cheek burned where he'd kissed it. In no way had it recovered. It had probably got, she thought fancifully, a printout right across it, saying how much she'd liked it…how much she liked *him*.

'This is the second time today we've eaten together.' Daniel's shoulder brushed hers as they sat side by side, their legs stretched out in front of them, their backs against James's car.

'So it is.' She affected surprise, tucking her hair behind her ears. 'I don't think, though, that Matron Brabazon would approve of all this junk food.'

'Good, isn't it?' He was munching happily.

'Brilliant!' she agreed. They finished everything, including the celery, even though they made a noise like horses munching. With both of them doing it, it didn't seem to matter. It compounded their companionship. Perhaps, Anna thought, the ultimate test of a good relationship is whether you can happily munch celery together. Not that they had a relationship as such, just a friendship with—occasionally—a burst of something else.

She took the plastic beaker of coffee he passed her,

and it went down in scalding gulps. Too much thinking had brought on awareness—awareness of him, of his long, masculine presence at her side. They sat in shadow, yet she could see every bit of him... Surely the stars overhead were as bright as the fairground lights.

'Perhaps,' she said shakily, 'we should join the others.'

'In a minute.' He reached for her empty beaker, setting it down to one side. Turning back to her, he cupped her face and bent to kiss her lips. She seemed to drown in sensation, sighing a little, opening her mouth under his. 'Oh, Anna, Anna, my lovely Anna!' Pressing her back on the grass, he kissed her eyes, her ears, her throat, fondled the curve of her breasts, his hands moving down the length of her body, over her abdomen and thighs. She ached for him, longed for him, wanting more and more.

When his hand ceased to move she couldn't bear it, but, alerted by a noise, he sat up, jerking out, 'I think we have company!' His words didn't sink in, didn't register clearly, until she saw, coming along by the swings, Julie and Sean, and Rowena and James bearing down on them.

'It was too crowded in there.' Julie waved a hand towards the marquee.

'Any coffee left?' James reached for the flask and Rowena and Sean collapsed on the grass beside Anna, Julie standing with Daniel who had sprung up at their approach. No one said anything, no one leg-pulled, but clearly they must have seen—not that it mattered, Anna was thinking, but she felt self-conscious just the same.

They made their way home after they'd eaten what remained of the food, the two cars parting company at the Fellingdon Bypass as they entered Seftonbridge. Seeing Daniel drive away at the wheel of the Metro, with Rowena and James in the back, Anna had the desolate feeling that he was speeding out of her life. I'm just tired, she thought, and I'm getting too fond of him…wanting him more and more.

'James mentioned Daniel's ex-wife tonight,' Julie remarked when they were getting ready for bed. 'He said she took him to a fair on Hampstead Heath once when he was about thirteen. He was at day school in south London then so he saw a fair bit of Daniel and her. He said she was fun, and gorgeous, and that he wouldn't be surprised if Daniel was still carrying a torch for her, which is why he's working himself to death, and buying houses and things.'

'Interesting,' Anna said jerkily, looking round at her friend, 'but it's the sort of thing a nineteen-year-old youth *would* say, isn't it? And it's quite probably way off-beam, but I know why you're telling me. You saw us, didn't you, in a clinch at the fair? That's what all this is about.'

'I saw a bit, not much. I saw Daniel getting up and I more or less guessed the rest.'

'It was a fun kiss at a fun fair. You don't need to warn me, Ju.'

'Better to know how the land lies, though, before you get in too deep.' Julie continued to the bathroom, her warning mission complete.

Anna creamed her face thoughtfully, wiped it clean on a tissue, but still sat there in front of the mirror, staring into it, seeing only a blur of white which was herself in a towelling robe.

It wasn't so much heed the gypsy's warning as heed my flatmate's, she thought. Julie meant well, and they *knew* each other well after three years of living together. If I had an affair with Daniel and it had to end, probably in a matter of weeks, I would be completely destroyed. It really would be like the end of the world—far worse than being dumped by Rob. It was this last fact, or realisation, that shocked her most.

I simply won't let it happen, she vowed as she got into bed, but it was a long time before she slept, and she could still, lying there in the dark, feel Daniel's hands moving down her body…and she longed for him to be there.

The ward on Monday looked entirely different without Mrs Ventnor in it. Her bed was occupied by a sixty-year-old patient who had been suffering from rheumatoid arthritis over a period of twenty-three years. She was in constant pain and had been admitted for a total knee replacement as she could now scarcely walk because of stiffness in the joint.

'Not to mention the pain, Sister,' she said to Anna during her round. 'Not that I'm not used to pain, but a little less would help!'

'I don't doubt that.' Ann smiled sympathetically, taking the time to explain all that was going to happen before the operation next day. 'You'll have the anaesthetist, and probably his nurse, coming to see you this morning. He'll want to listen to your chest and ask one or two questions, and you'll have a blood sample taken. During the afternoon Mr Mackay, your surgeon, will pay you a visit. The pre-operation period is a bit like holding court, Mrs Ashe. Everyone flocks to your side, promising the earth!'

'A new knee is all I ask, except, of course…' she gave a small grimace of pain as she made an unwary movement '…that a new joint where every joint is would be a good idea!'

It amazed Anna that she could joke at all, bearing in mind that she'd been taking anti-inflammatory drugs for years with no real relief from pain. There was a monkey-pole over her bed to assist movement, but she was unable to use it because of the pain and lack of strength in her shoulders and arms. 'I can roll,' she'd told the nurses when she'd been admitted yesterday, but even this would be impossible once she'd had surgery.

Kate Denver was down in the dumps as her knee-injury boyfriend had been discharged at the weekend. 'He said he'd come and visit me, but I don't suppose he will,' she said gloomily, manoeuvring about in her wheelchair with her 'metal leg' out in front. 'I think I'll get back on my bed now…not much point in going through there.' She indicated the day-room. 'I really do miss him, Sister. He was always good for a laugh.'

Anna positioned the wheelchair near to the bed, holding onto Kate's leg while she levered the rest of her slim shape safely onto the mattress.

In Mrs Pelly's old bed was a middle-aged patient due for mould arthroplasty. It had been explained to her that she would be having her operation just before twelve. She was a pretty woman, looking younger than the fifty years Anna knew she was.

'I keep telling myself that I'll be done and dusted by teatime,' she said, laying down her magazine as Anna approached, 'but that doesn't make me any less nervous. And even though Mr Mackay explained the whole procedure to me when I saw him in Outpatients, I'm still not sure what he meant by a mould.'

'It's a prosthesis, or cup, that's placed between the

knobbly part of your hip-bone and its socket,' Anna explained. 'Both the socket and end of the bone are shaped to exactly fit the cup. It stops the rubbing or grating that's causing your pain. You'll be able to move much more freely and feel safe as well.'

'So it's not a hip replacement—that's what confused me, you know.'

'No, nothing will be replaced. You'll keep what you've got, just have an extra bit fitted in.'

'Doesn't sound too bad when you put it like that!' Her eyes, big blue ones, Anna noticed, strayed to the clock on the wall. 'But I'm still nervous... Will you come with me—when they come for me, I mean?'

About to say that one of the nurses always accompanied the patient to Theatre, Anna changed her mind and promised that she would. 'I'll stay with you in the anaesthetic room until you're asleep.' She could fit her lunch in afterwards—take an early one, which would mean that she wouldn't be away from the ward any longer than usual. She might even catch a glimpse of Daniel down in Theatres... Not, of course, that this was her main reason for going, but it was an incentive, even so.

She gave Mrs Still her premedication at eleven o'clock. By then her knee had been marked, her identity-band checked with her medical notes and the laboratory reports that were to go with her to Theatre. On her locker, in a case like a jewel-box, reposed her contact lenses.

'My teeth are my own,' she said, proudly displaying them, 'so nothing to take out there!' Her hair had been pulled up under a cap, and she looked as most patients did in an operating gown that tied up at the back— slightly anonymous. She was more than a little sleepy when the porters arrived to wheel her, still on her bed, along to the theatre suite, Anna walking alongside.

At its entrance Anna donned overshoes and followed the little procession into the anaesthetic room. Even more sleepy now, Mrs Still managed a nod when Bob Tower, the anaesthetist, bent to speak to her.

'You'll just feel a little prick in your hand, Mrs Still, then away you'll go!'

It seemed to Anna, who was holding her other hand, that her eyes had a look of faint bewilderment before her lids dropped down. Once she was being intubated Anna turned to go. As she did so the door leading into the theatre swung open and she could see Daniel in his operating greens talking to Sister Beckham. They were laughing, plainly enjoying a joke. Behind them were ranged the rest of the team, all waiting for the patient who was just about to be wheeled in.

Feeling spare and decidedly *de trop*, Anna made her way out. Down here was Daniel's kingdom, this was where his real work was done. This was where Sister Beckham would see to all his wants, often through the ultimate in tense situations. I envy her, I'm even a little jealous of her, she thought, and was appalled.

'It's not often we see you in the theatre suite,' Daniel said, arriving on the ward at five o'clock just as Anna was preparing to go off.

'It was a special request from the patient. I like to oblige when I can,' she replied, keeping her voice light and managing to smile as well. So he had seen her, had he? Well, he might have managed a wave.

'There, now, I thought it was me you hoped to see!'

'Well, that, too…goes without saying!' It was best to compound the joke.

However, she was unable to look at him as she heard

him say, after a pause, 'Mrs Still's cup arthro went very well.'

'Yes, I saw from the theatre notes.'

'I'd like to see her charts, if I may, but don't let me hold you up.'

'Being held up isn't important.' She led the way into the ward, disappointing Jane who had seen him arrive and was longing to attend to him. Anna could see her at the ward desk, pointedly looking at her watch, no doubt trying to remind her about the duty overlap.

Mrs Still was asleep, her right leg on sliding skin traction, the pull of one and a half kilo weights keeping the limb still and preventing painful spasm. She looked corpse-like in the way of most patients after major surgery, which was why visitors were discouraged until at least the first night had passed.

'She'll be off traction in a fortnight, when she'll need careful passive hip exercises till her wound has healed.' Daniel handed her charts back to Anna, who replaced them at the end of the bed. Anna nodded, knowing that physiotherapy was especially important following cup arthroplasty.

As they left the bed Daniel crossed the aisle to speak to Mrs Ashe, due for knee replacement next day. 'This time tomorrow you'll have your new knee.' He smiled down at her. She was lying on her side and the nurses had placed a pillow between her legs to relieve strain on her muscles and joints.

'Rheumatoid arthritis is a terrible disease,' he said as they walked to the doors. 'No one has found a cure yet. All we can do is prescribe drugs and replace joints wherever possible. That poor woman will only be partially relieved after more pain from surgery and weeks of intensive physio.'

'She's looking *through* all that to the end result,' Anna told him. 'She says on the day she walks out of here she'll get a flag put up on the roof.'

'Nice woman.'

'Very.'

Their conversation lapsed, then, as Daniel held the corridor door back for Anna to pass through, he asked if she would do him a favour.

'Of course, if I can.' Anything, she thought, anything, anything. Just name it and its yours.

'It's about the house,' he said, and her hopes did a dive, along with the crowded lift which was taking them to the ground floor. 'I wondered if I could come along this evening, bringing my builder with me. If you and Julie are agreeable I would like him to look at your kitchen and give me a quote for converting it back into a bedroom, once the whole place is mine.'

'Yes, of course, come. I can't see any reason why not.' So that's all it was. Just building work, just a matter of pipes and plumbing and sink...not a personal favour at all.

'Strictly speaking,' he said, 'it's trespassing at this early stage, and I'm sure Mrs Court would think so.'

'It would be if you were downstairs in her part, but upstairs, as far as Julie and I are concerned, you come as our guest. While we're paying the rent we can call the tune.'

'Thanks, that's helpful.' They were in sight of his car lying alongside Bob Tower's Jaguar. As they drew level with it and he turned to get in, he swung round and faced her again. 'Anna, about Saturday night...'

'I enjoyed it,' she interrupted, stumbling over the words she had rehearsed over the weekend. 'I enjoyed being with you, well, I should think that was obvious, but I don't think it would be a good idea to take things any further.'

'For whom?' he asked quietly, confusing her. She had expected him to ask why not.

'It wouldn't be a good idea for me. I don't want an affair! I don't want an affair with anyone—it wouldn't work out for me!' I sound, she thought, like a sanctimonious little brat—me, me, me, all the way to the bank!

'In that case, we mustn't have one, must we?' He had his back to her now, unlocking the car, his long shadow thrown over its roof. 'Will six-thirty suit you and Julie—with Mr Speigler, I mean?' He slid behind the wheel and looked up at her, his eyes narrowed against the sun.

Anna nodded, turned away and walked over the tarmac. He didn't even, she thought, feeling upset, want to talk about what she had said. Most men would have wanted to know why she was determined to pull back. They would have tried to persuade her to go with the flow, or at least have been upset. Not so Daniel Mackay. He had settled for her decision as though he was more relieved than aggrieved. He doesn't want me on his conscience. He doesn't want to be encumbered with a recently dumped colleague who might want to cling too hard.

Julie and she ate their supper through in the sitting-room to give Mr Speigler and Daniel full rein in the kitchen. They could hear clicking and tapping as they consumed shepherd's pie and calabrese, Anna's going down in painful lumps. Closing the door on an affair with Daniel was having the effect of closing up everything else, even her throat.

'Anything happened between you two?' Julie jerked her head towards the door.

'We've just laid down a few ground rules.'

'*We?*' Julie's eyebrows rose.

'Well, *I* did, then!'

'Yes, well, you've probably been sensible, done the right thing for yourself. You're not an affair type.'

'Right now I wish I was.'

'Yes, of course you do, I can understand that. But you'll meet someone one day, Anna, who'll want you for keeps. If you'd had your fortune told on Saturday night, I'm sure that would have come up. Not that Rowena was all that chuffed with what *she* was told. When is she going out to Singapore?' Julie looked across at her friend.

'I think tomorrow.'

'I feel sorry for her. She'll hate leaving James.'

'Yes.' But Anna wasn't particularly interested in Rowena just at that moment. Her ears were tuned to the open doorway, where she could hear Daniel and Mr Speigler coming out onto the landing.

'All done and dusted, thanks!' Daniel's head appeared round the jamb. His glance included Julie but rested on Anna, who felt stuck to her chair. Mr Speigler was already descending the stairs.

'I'll see you out.' Julie half rose.

Thank God, Anna thought, she's not asking him to stay for coffee.

'No, don't get up.' He flapped a hand. 'I've disturbed you enough. Thanks again, both of you.' And with that he withdrew.

A few minutes later they heard the purr of his car moving off, followed by Mr Speigler's backfiring little van.

CHAPTER NINE

M<small>RS</small> A<small>SHE</small> made good progress following her knee replacement. There was no bleeding into the plaster and the two vacuum drains were able to be removed after forty-eight hours. Sir Guy, accompanied by Daniel, came to see her on her fourth day, the two surgeons arriving unexpectedly during afternoon visiting time.

Anna supposed they had to choose that time, but wished they hadn't. The ward had its full quota of visitors, including Mrs Barnes's terrible teenage twins, who were being noisy again—not that Sir Guy seemed to notice. His attention was all on his patient. It was Daniel who raised his eyebrows at Anna in a condemnatory kind of way, or at least she felt it was condemnatory. Perhaps he felt she ought to have gagged the little devils before letting them into the ward.

'You're doing wonderfully well, Mrs Ashe.' Sir Guy was straightening up from the bed. 'Not too much pain, I hope?'

'I'm used to it, as I told Sister the other day. A bit more doesn't make much difference!' This was said without a trace of self-pity. It was even said with a smile and thanks to both surgeons for all they'd done for her.

'Next week that plaster can be split and her sutures removed,' Sir Guy said at the desk. 'The back of it can be used as a splint when she's asleep or sitting out. If we find the wound has healed well she can be taken to the pool for hydrotherapy each and every morning. I hope to see her walking with a stroller three weeks from now.'

Before leaving the ward, he crossed the aisle to Mrs Barnes's plaster bed, telling her that in two weeks' time she would be X-rayed to see if bony union had taken place. 'If it has, you'll be lifted out of this contraption and be in a "human" bed again, with stabilising boards.'

'I'll tick off the days.' Mrs Barnes didn't smile. She was anxious about her son and daughter who, though momentarily quiet, were likely to break out again at any moment, and she was keeping her fingers crossed.

After looking at her charts, Sir Guy looked at them. 'Now, you two,' he said, looking down at them from his lofty height, 'are twins, if I'm not much mistaken. I've got a pair like you at home, but younger. Mine are ten. What are you—thirteen?'

'They're seventeen, sir,' Mrs Barnes supplied.

'Oh, really? You seem much younger.' He was looking straight at them again. 'Perhaps the way you were acting made me think that.' He paused, then added, 'A little noise doesn't matter, but an overload does.' This was said very pleasantly, almost conversationally, but when the surgeons left the bedside no cackle of laughter followed them.

'Wonders never cease,' Daniel remarked for Anna's ears alone, but she, like Mrs Barnes, was holding her breath.

Sir Guy, on the way out, mentioned his forthcoming party again, saying that he hoped they'd got their formal invitations. 'Charis has been busy sending them out.'

Anna's had come that morning, and she thanked him

for it, saying that she would reply in writing. 'I'm looking forward to it,' she said.

'Both Clive and I are invited,' Daniel told Anna after the consultant had gone, leaving him to sign a batch of prescriptions. 'One of us will have to be on call, which means that although we can both come, one of us might be called away just as the show livens up.'

'Who chooses the flip side?'

'I'll suggest to Clive that we toss for it. Seems the fairest way.'

And that, Anna thought, was decent of him, for having the senior position he could have pulled rank and merely decreed that Clive would be the one on call. As he handed over the signed prescriptions she very nearly told him that, nearly said that Clive should think himself lucky, but in the end she changed her mind and kept quiet, merely putting the scripts on one side for the pharmacy as he went out of the door.

There had been a slight change in his attitude ever since the night of the fair or, more precisely, since last Monday in the car park when she'd told him she didn't want an affair. Whereas before he had teasingly accepted her turn-downs, this time was different. This time he had pulled down a blind between them—no more than a thin curtain but a cut-off point just the same, like a line she dared not cross.

Clive, who missed very little, commented on it one day. 'You two had a spat?' he asked her, taking a KitKat off her teatray and tearing the wrapper off.

'Of course not—why?' She met his gaze, but he wasn't grinning for once.

'Just wondered.' He perched on the end of the desk, brushing wafer crumbs off his thigh. 'You *are* coming to the party a fortnight today, I trust?'

She nodded, looking down at the report she was try-ing to finish.

'I suggested,' he went on, 'that Daniel and I should toss for the on-call restriction.'

'*You* suggested?'

He had the grace to blush. 'Well, it might have been him. Anyway, I won. He'll come, but if someone breaks a bone in his absence he'll be whisked out and away.'

'I do know how these things work, Clive. Even I have to make sure that the ward is covered from seven until half past ten.' Anna got up to close the window against a sudden spatter of rain.

'See you there, then, like last year?'

'Yes.'

Clive was moving to the door much to Anna's relief. She couldn't think why he kept referring to last year, as though they'd been together all the time. She had, she remembered, played the field, and had had a won-derful time. It had been before she'd met Rob and she'd been looking for fun. She'd been free as air then.

She was free now, of course, but she didn't want to be. She wanted to be bound to Daniel, not for a few ecstatic nights but for all the days and nights to come in a lasting relationship. Daring to face this thought shook her. How could it have come about?

When Daniel asked her, on the Wednesday before the party, how she was getting there, she told him that her father would drive her. 'If I ask him nicely,' she said with a laugh.

'Ah, yes, of course.' He toed the carpet, his foot moving round a bald patch.

Lunches were being served in the ward. Anna could smell shepherd's pie, and her stomach rumbled, not for the pie but out of nervousness. He was still there, by the window now, looking down into the yard.

'I expect I shall walk from Maitland House. It's all but next door to Grange Road,' he said, and a faint hope died in her...

'Well, let's hope—' she forced herself to be glib '—that it keeps fine for you!'

He swung round from the window, and her heart skipped a beat. 'What I'd far rather do,' he jerked out, his hands deep in his pockets, 'is get the car out, but I was thinking about parking at the Morland residence, with twenty or thirty of us going.'

'Lots of people give others lifts, or at least they did last year. I don't remember there being any problem. Anyway, surely you'll need your car in case you're called out, and, yes, Clive *has* told me that you lost the toss!'

'Gleefully, no doubt!' He laughed, so did she.

'Well, a little, perhaps.'

'But you've convinced me. I'll take my car. In which case...' he inclined towards her slightly, bending from the waist '...I'll take you. I'll call round for you at Elvington Road. I don't think that five minutes of driving together will be likely to strain our cotton-wool relationship overmuch!'

She didn't pretend to misunderstand him, but she couldn't look at him either as he moved from the window to stand in front of her desk. All she could see was the white of his coat and his hands dangling from the sleeves.

'I don't think it would strain anything,' she said, 'and thank you very much.'

He looked surprised, she noticed, as their eyes made contact which, in turn surprised *her*, for he couldn't have thought she'd refuse, surely, but plainly he had. She must have hidden how she felt about him more efficiently than she'd realised—probably under those cotton-wool layers he'd just referred to.

You're beginning to love him…you *do* love him…so why don't you just stop playing safe and let it all happen? Let it all hang out, as Julie would say. The thought of this was so heady she didn't even see Daniel leave.

'What are you wearing?' Julie asked her, when she arrived home at six-thirty on the night of the party and found Anna in the bath.

'My cream dress.'

'Good choice, you'll wow them in that. It shows your shape but it's not too revealing. I mean, however good your boobs are you don't want them foaming over the top at the Morlands' annual do.'

'It's not a stuffy occasion. Charis Morland sees to that.' Anna began to dry herself, clearing the misty mirror and opening the window a crack.

'Still, it won't be like an office party, will it—all booze and snogging groups? Oh, by the way…' Julie changed tack. 'I've persuaded Sean to come with me to visit Mrs Pelly tonight. I've got her some of those marshmallows she likes and a single-dose bottle of gin.'

'Give her my love.' Back in her bedroom, in minuscule bra and pants, Anna was sliding the cream dress over her head. It was of cool, heavy silk and it clung to her curves as though it wanted to do nothing else. Her hair was upswept, she wore pearl drop earrings, and she looked as Julie said, like something off the front cover of *Elle*. She borrowed Julie's mohair stole in case the evening turned cool. She was cold at

the moment, but that was from nerves, waiting for the
doorbell to shrill. Outside in the street it was warm and
sunny.

Daniel arrived on the dot of seven-thirty, more
sharply black and white than ever in an impeccably cut
dark suit. Smart casual dress had been specified on the
invitation. Not every male on the ortho unit possessed
a dinner jacket, or wanted to hire one either. Anna's
dress was exactly knee-length, which was all in keeping, she felt.

'You look,' he said, as they drove down the road,
'like a princess.'

She laughed at this, her nervousness gone. 'Now, if
you'd said "fairy" princess I might have been
charmed.'

'It's the gold hair and hazel eyes. You look enchant-
ing. You'll have every red-blooded male prone at your
feet tonight.'

'They're all used to me. They see me every day.'

'Not in that dress they don't!'

'Oh, I see, so it's the wrapping that does it!'

'You know what I meant.' He sounded quite stern,
and she was silenced, not knowing how to gauge his
mood. He had a set look, and his jaw was tight, as was
the line of his mouth. Of course Sir Guy was his boss,
and meeting him socially, being a guest at his house,
wasn't perhaps the most relaxing occasion there was.

Fifteen minutes later, with the car safely parked in
the drive of The Beeches, Grange Road, they found
themselves in a group of thirty strong, most of whom
they knew. Sir Guy and Lady Charis were mingling
with their guests, trying to dispel the faint embarrassment that so often prevailed when colleagues were
gathered together in a non-working environment.

However as the drinks flowed, brought round by hired waiters, and as they all, at Sir Guy's suggestion, moved out into the garden, all awkwardness disappeared. Guests divided into groups, and Anna found herself standing on the sloping lawn with Pam Fiske, two women who were technicians from the labs, Clive, Sister Beckham and Mrs Parsons.

Mrs Parsons discoursed freely on the garden, which she seemed to know very well. 'All the houses on this side of the road run down to the river, you know.'

'That's probably why the grass is this rich lush green,' Angela Beckham put in. Out of her theatre garb she looked startling different, Anna observed. She was dark-haired with an urchin cut, which suited her pointed features, and her lipstick and nails matched her red dress and shoes. She was clearly enjoying herself. She and Daniel worked together in Theatres most days for long and tiring hours. They had their rest periods together, too, in the theatre suite coffee-room.

Swallowing hard against these thoughts, Anna looked around for Daniel, wishing he was with her instead of Clive, who was nudging against her and sliding his hand up her arm.

'Sir Guy seems to have commandeered Daniel,' Pam said. Anna's looking-round-for-Daniel gaze hadn't escaped her notice. 'Oh, there he is—look, over there.'

She moved aside, and there on the lower terrace were Sir Guy and Daniel, entertaining two other men whom Anna didn't recognise. She had just time to register that they weren't from the hospital when they began to traverse the lawn, and she saw that one of them—the stockily built, fair one—was Paul Ellison, the orthopaedic consultant from The Avenue Clinic.

As they came nearer, and before Daniel could intro-

duce him, Paul exclaimed at the sight of her, 'Surely
it's Anna Chancellor! Well, now, this *is* a surprise!' He
was plainly delighted, and Anna was flattered. It was
really quite something to be greeted so wholeheartedly,
and in front of all her peers. Not only that, but she was
glad to see him, glad to meet him again. He was a very
modest man, she remembered, almost self-effacing, but
most of all she remembered his kindness to her during
her fortnight at the clinic.

'It's lovely to see you,' she told him, smiling. 'Mr
Ellison and I met at The Avenue Clinic last April,' she
explained, mostly for Daniel's benefit but she included
the others as well.

Daniel, after introducing the second man—a surgeon
from Cletford Heath—walked off with him, rejoining
Sir Guy and his wife. Paul attached himself to Anna,
and more people joined their group, which in a way
gave them privacy and they were able to talk together.

'I've often wondered how you were getting on,
Anna. You're looking very much better.' What he
meant was that she was looking unutterably lovely, but
he wasn't given to eloquence.

'Oh, I am better, I'm fine!'

'It never crossed my mind that you'd be here at this
party!'

Anna laughed. 'Sisters are the lowest form of life
here tonight, but we made it, we three ward sisters, like
the witches in *Macbeth*!'

'So glad you did.' Paul spilled a little of his drink.
'Could we, perhaps, sit over there?' He indicated a
group of chairs below the terrace which so far remained
empty.

'I don't see why not.' Where had Daniel got to? Why
couldn't Sir Guy leave him alone?

It was fast becoming dusk and the little lamps on the terraces had been switched on, leaching the colour from the climbing roses so they all appeared white and making the wisteria dripping from the orangery roof resemble an army of ghosts...or wraiths...or spectres. For some reason Anna shivered and reached for her stole.

'You're not cold?' Paul enquired.

'No, just a goose walking over my grave! I'm always shivering and shuddering—it must be in my genes!'

He didn't laugh as she'd intended...as *she* was doing, laughing at her own joke. But, then, he wasn't, as she was beginning to remember, a man who laughed easily. All the same, she was happy to be with him and to hear all his news. He told her that he had recently been to France. 'I stayed with my late wife's parents, you know, who retired to Antibes. They like to talk about Angela and Tom, which is very natural, of course.'

Angela had been Paul's wife, Tom his six-year-old son. They had been killed in a road accident on Christmas Eve two years ago. He had told Anna about it one day when she'd been nursing at the clinic. She had told him of her own troubles, their confidences coming easily because they were strangers, and because neither cared what each thought of the other...at least that was how it had seemed to Anna at the time.

'You know, I always thought,' Paul was saying to her now, 'that that fiancé of yours would come back and *beg* you to marry him.'

'At first,' Anna said frankly, 'I hoped that he would, but not now, not any longer. I've moved on, as they say.'

'I can see that for *you* that wouldn't be difficult.'

'Meaning that I'm fickle?' she teased.

He was instantly horrified. 'No, no, of course not! I meant that it's more difficult for me. I'm older, for one thing.'

'Not by much!'

'By a dozen years at least.' She made no comment, and he went on. 'To find the right partner isn't easy, especially the second time round. Inevitably one makes comparisons, I think, but, yes, I admit I would like to marry again and have a second family, but sometimes I think that's a pipe dream.'

Anna had no time to reply before they were descended on by a crowd wanting chairs and interrupted by Sir Guy announcing that supper was being served in the house. Someone near Anna, who turned out to be Clive, muttered, 'About time, too.'

'Shall we go in, Anna?' Paul offered an arm to her. 'But, of course, you may be with someone. I'm afraid I just assumed…'

'I'm not with anyone special, no. Just going with the flow tonight!' A little high on two glasses of wine, Anna slipped a hand through his arm.

Behind a long damask-clothed table in the Morlands' garden room caterers were serving out game pie, quiches and cooked meats. Salads abounded, and bowls of strawberries, raspberries and cream lent colour to the scene.

'Home-grown,' Sir Guy intoned. 'Likewise the peaches, picked from the orangery only hours ago.'

Most people carried their plates out to the terrace, including Anna and Paul, the balding doctor from Cletford, Daniel and Sister Beckham, and Clive Stone, who all sat down in a group. The talk ranged from culinary programmes on television to the millennium celebrations. The NHS was delicately touched on then dropped by mutual accord. Anna never knew how they got onto property, but somehow or other they did, Daniel, who'd contributed little up to then, saying that he'd been lucky enough to find a handsome terraced property in Elvington Road that suited him down to the ground.

'Good area.' Paul looked interested. 'Property will hold its value there. Wasn't that where you were living, Anna?' He moved his plate off his knees with care and turned to look at her. Daniel was looking, too, as was Clive.

Feeling somehow forced into a corner, she said, 'In the same house. It's that one Daniel's buying. I'll need to move pretty soon.'

'Alas, these thing happen, don't they?' Clive was enjoying himself.

'Have you found somewhere else to live?' Paul enquired.

'No, I'm going home for a time to my parents' hotel, then I'll flat-search from there.'

'There's no rush, Anna knows that. I'm not exactly turning her out.' Daniel's glance at her was a little spiked, and she was just about to agree and admit there was no question of that when Sir Guy appeared behind his chair.

'Sorry, Daniel, call from A and E. You're in demand, I'm afraid!'

'Just my luck! Still, I've finished my supper!' As he got up Sir Guy took his chair. Anna half rose, jogging Paul's arm.

'What rotten luck, Daniel. I'm so—'

'I'll come back if I can,' he said lightly, smiling

round at them all, then made his way swiftly round the side of the house to where he'd left the car.

'Name of the game.' Clive smirked, and Anna looked daggers at him.

Daniel *did* get back, two hours later, when everyone was preparing to leave. Anna, who'd been asked to share a taxi with Pam and three of the laboratory staff, excused herself and drove home with him.

'I was determined to collect you if I could,' he said as they moved down the drive in the wake of the other cars.

'I'm glad.'

'Are you?'

'Yes, of course I am. What was it, an accident case?'

'An RTA, yes. Young boy with multiple injuries, ribs piercing a lung. The thoracic team could have coped without me, to my mind, but, still, that's the way it goes.'

'I'm glad you'd eaten before you went.'

'Ah, yes, talking of which—' they were on the main road now and gathering a little speed '—I was shocked to hear you tell Paul Ellison that you weren't with anyone special, just going with the flow. That's a fine way to dismiss your chauffeur for the night!'

'Oh, *dear*!' Anna went hot.

'Exactly,' Daniel said.

'I didn't mean it to sound the way it came out, and I didn't—' she was trying to laugh '—know you were near.'

'I believe that part, but not the first. I think you meant it all right.' He had been joking at first, but now he wasn't. He was stern behind the wheel, not driving recklessly but faster than he should have been. Anna felt it behoved her to be quiet until they were clear of the town, when she ventured to say, because she didn't want bad feelings between them, 'I thought you wanted to circulate, anyway, not be stuck with me.'

'Unfortunately…' he dropped his speed as they approached the roundabout '…Sir Guy had me singled out as a kind of second host, which was flattering in a way, I suppose, but not what I had in mind.'

This was true, Anna realised, *and* he'd been called out. 'You haven't had much of an evening, have you?' she sympathised.

'Not really, no, but what about you?' he asked a little more equably.

'I enjoyed myself. There was dancing after supper out on the terrace.' She would have enjoyed herself more if he had been there, but somehow or other she couldn't find a way of telling him that, not in his present mood. In any case, he was changing the subject and asking if the next weekend was when she and Julie were moving out.

'Yes, Julie leaves for Ireland on Sunday week,' she said, 'and I'm going home, as you know. But tonight, believe it or not, I was told about a flat.'

'Oh, really? Where?' He glanced sharply at her as they breasted Magdalene Bridge.

'In Bateman Street, near the botanical gardens. Paul Ellison's mother wants to let part of her house—the top part, like Mrs Pelly. She's understandably nervous about it, wondering who she will get. Paul is looking out for someone and says he will recommend me. If I like it, it may solve my problem. It may be just the thing. I don't want to live at home in the long term, much though I love Mum and Dad.'

'I see.' The two words dropped like stones into the near-silent purring of the car. Too late Anna realised she was on very dangerous ground. 'So,' Daniel went on, just as heavily, 'you reject my offer to stay on in your present flat, but are perfectly happy—in fact, keen—to consider one from him. I could see he was all over you from tonight.'

'That's simply not true!'

'Oh, I think it is!'

'But I hardly know the man, and the flat arrangement, if it comes to anything, is a business deal, and anyway…' Angered by his silence, she burst out, 'I'm a free agent, I can do what I like. You don't own me, you know!'

The car had stopped outside the house, and her seat belt strap went zinging back. Ducking her head, she made to get out and wish him goodnight all in one, but he wasn't having that, and she felt him grip her arm.

'For God's sake, Anna!' He pulled her round on the seat. His hand gently but firmly brought her face to his, and she saw the glint of his eyes in one harsh second before his mouth crushed hers.

She felt the anger in him, and the passion. She felt it rising in herself, as their tongues met, and explored, and tangled, his hand finding her breasts over the top of the cream silk dress, and as his leg thrust between hers she found herself moving against him, little cries escaping her.

It was he who broke away first, moving back from her as the lights of an approaching car streamed over them. Half-blinded and breathless, Anna got out and was at the gate, fumbling for the latch, before he got to her side. 'You don't have to run from me. Making love in cars isn't something I normally—'

'Oh, leave it…just leave it… Leave me alone!'

'Send me the bill for your dress.'

'It doesn't matter!'

'It does to me!' He was stiff now, standing with his head held high. What she wanted was to be held again, something tender said in her ear but, having unlocked the door for her, he had half turned to move away. She said goodnight and so did he, practically at the same moment, then off he went down the brick path, while she went in and closed the door.

Julie was in bed, but not asleep. 'Hey, come in. I want to hear all about it,' she called, when Anna would have passed by her door. There was nothing for it but to show herself, otherwise Julie would have come out. So in she went and waited for the comments, which came thick and fast. 'Heavens, Anna, you look as though you've been raped!'

'Well, I haven't.'

'Your dress is torn.'

'I know it is.'

'Who brought you home?'

'Daniel, of course.' Shivering slightly, Anna sank down on a stool. 'It's been quite an evening,' she said in a wobbly voice.

'I can see that for myself!' Julie was getting out of bed in her striped men's pyjamas. 'I'm going to make you a mug of hot chocolate, and you can tell me about it—or not tell me, just as you like.'

In the end all Anna said was that the evening had been fun, but that she'd upset Daniel on the way home and things had got out of control. Julie asked no more questions, she didn't need to. She could fill in the gaps. She could sew, too, and while Anna drank her chocolate she mended the neck of the dress so finely and skilfully, and with such tiny stitches, that the tear didn't show.

CHAPTER TEN

NOT having slept until daybreak, Anna was still asleep at nine, not that this mattered for she was on late duty and had plenty of time to get ready to face the day, which meant facing Daniel, too. Don't, she prayed as she set off, let him mention last night. On the other hand, don't let him go all cold on me, as though he's blotting it out.

It was a hot morning and Princes Parade sweltered in the noonday sun. While the leaves of the giant chestnut tree in front of the Senate House hung dark and limp, college buildings and pavements baked in golden light.

By the time Anna got to the hospital she was pretty baked herself. She was glad to step into A and E's antiseptic coolness, and as she sailed up in the lift her usual calm asserted itself. The first thing she saw as she entered her office was the bouquet of flowers on her desk—pink and white carnations and stocks, with a little card attached. Her heart lifted. They were from Daniel, they had to be! The envelope holding the card had 'Flowers for Sister Chancellor' scrawled boldly across it, but not in Daniel's writing. Then who...? With feverish fingers she pulled out the card and read, 'With many thanks for your company last evening, Paul Ellison.'

Anticlimax, disappointment, hit her like a blow. She was still battling with it when a sound made her turn to see Daniel coming in with Jane, the latter devoid of her usual confident air.

'You'll have heard, of course!' Daniel was crossing over to the filing cabinet.

'Sister has only just come on duty, Mr Mackay.' Jane ranged herself at Anna's side.

'What is it? What's happened?'

Miss Arkwright's notes were being dropped onto the desk. 'This patient fell in the ward half an hour ago.' Daniel's finger stabbed at the notes. 'She's done some damage—dislocated her hip—which means opening her up again. I'd like her down in Theatres at three so get Bob Tower up straight away, and go in and see her, please. She's naturally upset.' All this was said with his head down as he wrote in the notes.

'But how did it happen?' This can't be happening, Anna thought.

Jane started to explain, but Daniel waved her to silence. 'You can go into all that when I've gone. And it's all right, Nurse. I know you're short-staffed and none of you have got eyes in the back of your heads.'

Jane went off thankfully to supervise ward lunches. 'If you'd been here it wouldn't have happened.' Daniel was still busy writing, and his remark to Anna's sensitised ear wasn't so much a compliment as a grouse that she hadn't been on duty. Even so, she could understand how he was feeling. Rebecca Arkwright had made rapid progress after her arthroplasty which had been performed by Daniel twelve days ago. Right from day one she had put her back into getting well, never failing to practise her exercises, eagerly graduating from elbow crutches to two sticks and then to one stick for the last two days. Now, poor woman, she was back to the starting post again.

With all this on board Anna had forgotten that her flowers were still on the desk. With a little pang of dismay she saw that Daniel had picked up the card. 'Hmm, nice gesture,' he said. 'Nice flowers too. Better get them in water, hadn't you, or they'll wilt in all this heat?' He made to replace the card, dropped it, swore then picked it up. Thrusting it amongst the sprouting ferns, he moved towards the door. 'Three o'clock for Miss Arkwright, remember…'

I'm hardly likely to forget, Anna thought, and as he breezed up the corridor she reflected that she needn't have worried that he'd mention last night. The ward and its traumas had drawn a tight cover and seal over personal matters. Smoothing down the front of her dress, she went into the ward.

'It was no one's fault but mine, Sister,' Rebecca Arkwright said. 'I got out of bed to go to the loo. Nurse Scott helped me—handed me my stick and off I went. I was all right in the loo, but when I was halfway back I realised I'd left my stick in there and panicked. I literally froze. I couldn't go back for it, and I couldn't move forward, I could see my bed, but I was too frightened to move towards it and then…well, I just fell, and there was this awful pain.'

'I can't think why I didn't notice her coming in from the loo.' The physiotherapist, Helen Shaw, came over from the desk. 'I was working on Kate Denver, only three beds up!'

'Mr Mackay said the operation wouldn't take as long as last time.' Rebecca looked at her leg, lying between sandbags, her face drawn with pain.

'That's true,' Anna said, thinking to herself, not the actual surgery, perhaps, but getting over it, becoming mobile again, would be very much the same. Not that she was going to tell Rebecca that—at least not today.

Back in the office Jane was in tears. 'I was in charge, Anna, and I was standing right here with the door open when she came out of the loo! I should have seen her, or waited in there with her—it's all my fault!'

Reassuring so many people was wearing Anna out. It was putting her behind with her paperwork, too, so when Pam Fiske came to take her to lunch she shook her head. 'Bring me a sandwich when you come back, Pam, any sort but beef, and if there's a banana or an apple, I'll have that, too.'

'You need to come up and have a proper break.' Pam made a fuss as Anna had known she would. 'Besides, I want to talk about the party.'

'No can do,' she said. 'We've had an accident on the ward.'

'Yes, I know. I heard about it probably before you did. All right, then, I'll bring your grub down just this once.' Fully in the room now, she caught sight of Anna's flowers. 'What a gorgeous bouquet—must have cost the earth. Is it for a patient?' She was trying to smell the flowers over the top of the Cellophane.

'They're from Paul Ellison,' Anna said shortly.

'*Are* they indeed?' Pam looked at the open card, just as Daniel had done. 'He's a friend of the Morlands'— helped Sir Guy out here in Theatres when he had flu. He's what you might call the conventional type—worthy, but dull.' After this little spiel she relinquished the flowers, and went off to the canteen.

With the ward lunches out of the way, Jane came in with the afternoon-shift nurses to give the handover report. Rebecca Arkwright had her premed injection during the quiet hour, and at five minutes to three ex-

actly was wheeled down to Theatres. By then visiting
was in full swing, friends and relatives drifting in from
the hot streets in sundresses and shorts. By the time
the evening batch arrived Rebecca was back in the
ward, and at eight-thirty Daniel appeared.

'I'll just take a peep at her charts,' he said, moving
quietly to her bed as some patients were already asleep
and settled for the night. 'Keep the infusion running
for the next couple of days, and her leg in a trough for
the time being until I see her again. And let's just
hope,' he added, as they walked into the corridor, 'that
some rightly indignant relative doesn't sue us for neg-
ligence. She has a mother, doesn't she?'

'Yes, her next of kin, she's over ninety. Apparently
when Jane rang her to tell her about the accident, she
said she wasn't surprised as Rebecca had always "been
a one for falling" when she was a little girl!'

'Good Lord!' Daniel laughed.

Encouraged by this, Anna went on, 'She comes in
to visit, and is amazingly agile, doesn't use a stick. I
would imagine she is a bit of a tartar, though. I dare
say Rebecca is finding being in here something of a
rest. I'm not saying it's not unfortunate that—' She
broke off as Daniel all but pushed her into the office
and closed the door with a click. She felt a tingle of
warning, or was it thrill, for what was coming?

'At the risk of embarrassing you,' he began steadily,
his back against the door, 'I meant what I said about
letting me have a bill for mending your dress.'

'Oh, that old thing.' She managed to laugh. 'It's
done. Julie mended it.'

'*Julie?*' Up went his brows.

'Yes, last night, and, no,' she went on as his expression hardened, 'I didn't give her a graphic account

of how it came to be torn, but obviously she guessed. She'd have had the nous to realise it got damaged in the heat of the moment—*mutual* heat. After all, if our clinch had gone on much longer, I might have ripped your shirt!'

'I wish you had, but I don't think *you* wish it! Titillating remarks are easy to bring out in safe surroundings, where there can be no comeback.' He moved closer to her, eyes intent, his mouth beginning to smile. When she jerked back, mindful of the wide viewing window, he laughed and opened the door. 'I rest my case, Sister Chancellor,' he said, and quietly left the room.

They met again the next afternoon, Saturday, when she and Julie went to visit Mrs Pelly and pay her their final week's rent. Anna almost jumped at the sight of Daniel sitting there, long and dark in fawn chinos and a spanking white shirt, his black hair curving over its collar, his face turned towards the door.

Julie was the first to speak. 'Hope we're not interrupting,' she said.

'Oh, how lovely to see you!' Mrs Pelly tried to get up when Daniel did, but Anna pressed her back in her chair. She and Julie sat on the bed in the absence of any more chairs, Julie explaining that she'd come to say goodbye as she was off to Ireland the following weekend.

'We're going to live in Dublin's fair city, Sean and I!'

'You'll miss her, won't you, dear?' Mrs Pelly looked at Anna. 'It's a long way away.'

'From Seftonbridge, yes,' Anna agreed.

'But she'll come and visit us—it's not *all* that far

away, really.' Julie looked momentarily doubtful, chewing on her underlip.

'Not as far away as Singapore,' Daniel put in, 'from where, if you believe it, Rowena rings James every single night.'

'Someone's going to get a big phone bill,' Anna said, and everyone laughed, including Daniel, which made her feel easier.

'Talking of money.' Anna handed Mrs Pelly a cheque. 'That's our very last rent for the flat. We told Mrs Court we'd be bringing it along today.'

'Ah, yes, I always had the rent, you know,' the old lady told Daniel. 'That was the arrangement Doris and I had when I made over the house. It's been a good afternoon for business.' She handed the rent book back to Anna. 'Mr Mackay and I have just agreed a price for the furniture so I'm feeling quite rich.'

Tea was brought in at this point, nicely set out on a tray with little cakes in paper cases, two for each of them. 'The food is very good here.' Mrs Pelly watched Anna pour out. 'And we're well looked after, *very* well looked after, but, of course, it's not like home.'

There was an awkward silence, which Daniel broke as he peeled the paper off his cake. 'With the best will in the world, Mrs Pelly, I think you would have found that as time went on you would have found it harder and harder to manage on your own. As we get older, and it happens to all of us—or does if we're lucky— we need people round us more. We need to feel that help is at hand.'

Mrs Pelly neither agreed nor disagreed with this, just looked thoughtful till Julie said, 'It'll be a wrench for all of us on Saturday, especially for Anna. She sort of bonded with the house right from the very start.'

'Which I did as well.' Mrs Pelly put her hand over Anna's. 'Of course, it was never the same after my husband died, so I expect you're right.' She was looking at Daniel now. 'It's time for me to move on.'

Out on the forecourt half an hour later Daniel offered the two of them a lift home.

'We're not going home,' Julie told him, pirouetting on her heel. 'We're making the most of our last weekend together and going to see *Shakespeare in Love*. Afterwards we're having a meal at the University Arms. We girls know how to enjoy ourselves!'

'That I can believe.' Daniel laughed, looking towards his car. 'So you don't want a lift, then?'

'Yes, we do, to the town centre,' Julie said before Anna could speak. In they got and five minutes later they were being set down at the cinema in Regent Street, where they joined a sizeable queue.

'You've got an awful cheek,' Anna told Julie after Daniel had driven away. 'He might have had something else on.'

'If he had he wouldn't have been visiting Mrs Pelly, or offered to drive us home. And another thing,' she said more quietly as they shuffled forward in the queue. 'Now that I know him better I think you could do far worse than have a full-blown affair with him. So, OK, he's not for long-term commitment, but he *is* a caring man. He wouldn't just dump you like that Robert Dudley did!'

'So, what's good about being let down lightly?' Anna queried. 'And I don't think this is the sort of conversation to be having in a queue!'

What she didn't say was that she had already come to the same conclusion as Julie. It was high time she stopped being so cautious and self-protective. She loved Daniel and wanted him madly, she was painfully aware of that. At the very first opportunity she was going to tell him that she felt the same way as he did about a closer relationship.

The opportunity didn't present itself, though, and it took far greater nerve than Anna possessed to make the first move. There *were* ways, but lack of confidence held her back. She could, for instance, have rung Daniel up early on Sunday and asked him to the flat for lunch. Julie would have been there, but she'd have been off with Sean later on. Anna thought about it, rehearsed little inviting speeches all that night, but in the end did nothing, in case he turned her down.

On Monday he was in Theatre all day and didn't come to the ward at all, but on Tuesday, just as breakfasts were out of the way, she had word that Sir Guy and he would be doing a ward round, starting at ten o'clock. There followed the usual rush to assemble everything, and just at the height of it the pharmacist arrived to do his three-monthly spot-check of the drugs. He and his assistant carried out their meticulous task, finishing only a matter of minutes before the two surgeons arrived.

The round was to be a business one, not a teaching one, which meant there were no medical students.

Anna's and Daniel's greetings to one another were by necessity perfunctory. Sir Guy, however, delayed enough to tell Anna how pleased he and his wife had been to see her on Friday night. 'Charis wanted to take you up to see the baby,' he said, 'but I told her you were with us to enjoy yourself, not make the acquaintance of a drooling infant, charming though she is.'

Anna, only too conscious of Daniel by her side, replied to the effect that she would have loved to have seen Emily. 'She must have grown tremendously over the past twelve months.'

After this little exchange they went into the ward, Anna leading the way, her eye doing a quick scan over the two lines of beds. Helen, the physio, standing by the central desk, was to join them this morning as Sir Guy wanted to see the more mobile patients being put through their paces.

Mrs Ashe professed herself delighted with her new knee. She had been having daily trips to the hospital pool, doing exercises under water, as well as different ones in the ward. Helen had now got her knee to bend to ninety degrees, and she was able to walk a few paces with a rollator, as Sir Guy had hoped.

'Well done,' he told her, his smile including Helen. 'You've worked hard together and come up with a good result. The next step is to get you assessed in the occupational therapy department. They'll be able to tell Mr Mackay and me when you're able enough to manage at home.'

The scoliosis patient, Mrs Barnes, had progressed very slowly. Out of her plaster shell and in an orthopaedic bed, she had been having strengthening exercises with Helen and could now sit up. 'After three months of staring at the ceiling, it's like a brand-new view of life. I just can't stop looking round,' she told them as they chatted by her bed.

'Next week we'll have you standing,' Sir Guy promised. 'Then, once you get your balance back, the next stage will be walking. How do you feel about that?'

'A little scary, but I'm dying to try it. My twins will be thrilled. They'll think it's wicked,' she said, looking at Anna and Daniel, who laughed, while Sir Guy, not fully comprehending, shook his head in puzzlement.

Mrs Barnes's latest X-ray films were studied on the display box, Anna signalling to Kate Denver that she would be the next to be seen.

Kate, although delighted to be walking again, was finding her functional brace cumbersome. She wasn't yet used to the weight of it, and kept hitting and bruising her good leg with the hinge. Also, walking with elbow crutches, she was inclined to favour the mended limb. 'You can put your full weight on it,' Daniel had told her, and Sir Guy backed him up. 'Your crutches are for balance. Your leg needs to be used as naturally as possible. Once you can flex the knee and manage stairs, we can think of discharging you.'

Rebecca Arkwright, the 'fallen' hip replacement patient, was seen nearly last. Now on her fourth postoperative day, she had been encouraged to walk again, but she was far more nervous than she had been first time round.

'That's the great pity of accidents,' Sir Guy said back in the office. 'The patient loses his or her nerve...very regrettable.' He said no more than that, and only the merest wisp of blame hung in the air as he lowered himself into a chair, which Anna cleared for him in the nick of time.

She wondered why he seemed bent on staying, but as he did she couldn't very well leave him and go into the ward to supervise lunches. 'You're going to have to make do with me and Clive until next week,' he said. 'Daniel has agreed to stand in for me at the international ortho conference, in London, as from tomorrow.'

'Oh, I see.' Anna flicked a glance at Daniel, who was looking rather pleased at the prospect of three days, plus a weekend, in Town. It was a well-known fact, she knew, that conference delegates had a fair bit of free time. He would probably look up that girlfriend, or girlfriends, he was reputed to have, they would take in a show, go clubbing and all the rest of it. Hadn't he once said that being in London gave him a buzz?

'Where are you staying?' she asked without thinking, and caught Sir Guy's surprised glance.

'Friends of mine have a flat in the Barbican,' Daniel said, smiling at her.

'Ah, yes, talking of flats…' Sir Guy was getting up at last. 'I understand, Anna, that you may be renting one in Elizabeth Ellison's house. She's a charming old lady, easy to get on with. Paul worries about her being on her own, with him two miles across town. I hope it all comes to fruition, for her sake, his *and* yours. Paul told me, by the way, that you did sterling work at the clinic a few months back.'

'I enjoyed being there, up to a point,' Anna said carefully.

'Not enough to want to nurse in the private sector permanently, I hope?' Sir Guy made for the door in a rush, without waiting for her reply. He had just remembered he was supposed to be meeting a young American professor in biochemistry at noon.

It looked to Anna as though Daniel was bent on following him out, but he turned at the door and asked her how she and Julie had enjoyed *Shakespeare in Love*.

'Oh, we loved it, we both did!' Don't let him rush off for a few minutes, she prayed.

'I'll make a point of seeing it when I'm in Town.'

'I'm sure you'll like it.' Desperate to keep him, she asked when he'd be back.

'Some time on Sunday, probably late. I may as well,' he continued smoothly, 'pack in all I can.'

'Yes.'

And now he really was going. She had no reason or excuse to stop him, except one, of course, but she could hardly blurt out that he should come back on Friday night and they'd spend the weekend together in his flat at Maitland House.

'I hope everything goes well for you on Saturday,' he said. 'Moving out, I mean, and saying goodbye to Julie. I'm sorry about it, you know.' He had come back to the desk and was standing in front of it.

'No need to have a conscience about it.' She spoke more sharply than she'd intended. 'If you hadn't bought the house, someone else would have, sooner or later, and Julie would have gone to Ireland, anyway... *C'est la vie*, as they say!'

He said, quite briefly, 'Bye, then.' And he was gone.

I handled that terribly badly, Anna thought. Instead of encouraging him, I'm pushing him away. I seem to be losing out on all fronts.

And it was certainly a feeling of loss, leaving Elvington Road on Saturday morning in the hotel van her father had sent to collect her and Julie's things. They sat in the back with their suitcases and bags, looking out of the porthole windows and feeling sad. Julie's sadness, however, was the transient kind, for she was going to Sean. 'Pigging it in his bedsit till Sunday night,' she said.

She was dropped off at a house in Fenton Street, where Sean, all smiles, was waiting out on the pavement to take her cases up the stairs. 'Don't forget, you're both coming to dinner tonight,' Anna called out from the van.

'We won't.' Sean was still grinning.

Lois and Edward Chancellor were at the hotel entrance to give Anna a five-star welcome. Her father's hug brought tears to her eyes, which she knew was ridiculous, but it was an emotional morning. It was a pity, she thought, that she wasn't on duty, which would have cured her once and for all.

She spent the morning unpacking in the room in the family flat that had always been hers. From its window she could look down on Ackamore's Boat Yard, where the waterman was already doing a brisk trade in hiring out punts. Most people—unless they were practised punters—opted for paddles instead of a pole. There was a man and a girl setting off now, taking a paddle apiece.

Anna wondered what Daniel was doing. He wouldn't be back until tomorrow. She wondered who his friends in the Barbican were. Perhaps they were friends he'd made when he was at St Mildred's, London Bridge, or perhaps it was just one friend—a woman. She was biting hard on that when her mother appeared in the room, asking if she'd like to brave the Saturday crowds and go out on a shopping spree.

'I can do with another evening skirt,' she said, 'and I'll treat you to whatever you like—barring Versace, of course!'

So that's what they did, and at four o'clock, with their purchases stowed under a table in the Coffee House in Regent Street, they ate a Danish pastry apiece and rested their feet.

'I suppose,' Lois said, looking out at the sea of passing shoppers, 'we're not likely to run into that Mack-the-Knife friend of yours?'

'If you mean Daniel Mackay, he's in London.' Anna

cut into her pastry. 'He's been taking Sir Guy's place at a conference, and he's due home tomorrow. I'm surprised you remember him. You only saw him in a flash when he nearly ran you down!'

'A flash was enough. Besides, you introduced me— a stunning young man. You know, Anna...' Lois eyed her daughter carefully. 'Living at home doesn't mean you can't ask your friends round. Dad and I won't be breathing down your neck all the time.'

'Thanks.' Anna was tempted to mention the flat in Bateman Street but she didn't because for one thing, she didn't know if she wanted to pursue it. Instead, she changed the subject and reminded her mother that they hadn't yet bought the food.

'No, we haven't. We'd better get along to Markersons now. I thought whitebait, followed by duck, then raspberry pavlova and some of that feta cheese Julie likes.' Lois looked at Anna for her approval.

'Sounds great to me,' she said. 'It's the last decent meal they'll have before flying off tomorrow. I'm glad we're having it in the flat—I think they'll like that better.' And I'll have to be cheerful all through it, she thought, not sitting there all glum-faced.

'We'll have champagne, too,' Lois said on the way to the supermarket, 'to wish them well in their new life.'

Nodding, Anna agreed.

In the end it was the kind of friendly gathering that went off with a bang. The champagne was an inspiration, turning what could have been a strained-and-tinged-with-sadness occasion into a celebratory one.

'Here's to a bright new future for Julie and Sean.'

Edward Chancellor had got to his feet, raising his glass on high.

Sean replied, thanking him, and hard on the heels of that, Julie proposed a toast of her own. 'To Anna,' she said, 'the best friend a girl ever had. I can't wait for her to visit us in Dublin. We shall never ever lose touch.'

There were quick goodbyes in the drive later, stiff faces and convulsive hugs, and then the happy couple were off. Anna watched them drive away in the softly falling dusk.

She spent the greater part of Sunday sketching and painting, sitting at the open window of her room where she could get, as well as a view of the river crowded with canoes and punts, a more distant one of the water-meadows and the spire of St Martin's church. The solitary creative activity concentrated her mind, yet relaxed her, too, and built up her confidence, enabling her to make plans. She wouldn't, she decided, go further into the matter of taking the Bateman Street flat. She would tell Paul that she had decided to live at home for the time being.

As she made her decision she was mindful of her mother's insistence that she must ask friends home. She would, therefore, take courage and ask Daniel to supper one night. 'My parents would love to meet you again…it might be fun.' There she was, rehearsing little speeches again, but this time she would use them for real.

The rather oppressive heat of the day lingered on into the evening, and at ten o'clock there were still one or two guests strolling about in the grounds. The traffic on the river had subsided long since, for no craft was hired out after dusk, but couples still walked along the towpath, and lovers still lay in the grass farther upriver by Coe Fen and the women's bathing huts. Anna, with her father, was in the vegetable garden, helping him close the vents in the greenhouses in case there was a storm in the night. Tomatoes hung heavy and ripe from the vines.

'We'll have a glut if this weather keeps on,' Edward said, linking his arm in his daughter's as they circled the grounds to the waterfront side where they sat on a seat at the top of the sloping lawn, trying to catch a breeze.

'I suppose,' Edward went on when they were settled, taking a swipe at a hanging cluster of gnats, 'you'll be cycling off soon after seven tomorrow morning?'

'Actually, no.' Anna smiled at him. 'I'm not on duty till half past twelve. I'm usually on lates on Mondays and Fridays. I try to be fair when I do the rosters. It's not all honey, being a ward sister, you know!'

'I bet you're the best ever.' Edward swiped at the gnats again. 'Dratted things, nip like the devil,' he was saying, just as an ambulance, its siren wailing, tore by on the opposite side of the river behind the trees in Telford Way, a police car following closely.

Anna's blood chilled. There must have been an in-cident…an accident upriver! Running down the slope, she could just make out the vehicles' lights as they turned in at the bridge.

'See anything?' her father puffed, joining her at the rail.

'No…too far up… Seems to be at the bridge.'

'Pack of youngsters most likely, messing about,' her father growled, and she shuddered, remembering the day she'd seen the boy on the parapet wall.

'Well, there's nothing we can do. I'll hear about it

soon enough tomorrow, I expect,' Anna said as they moved up the lawn again. But the peace of the garden seemed somehow invaded, the more so when a second ambulance sirened its way upstream. 'Heavens above!' She clutched her father's arm.

'Doesn't look too good, does it?' Even he felt a sense of shock.

'Let's go in. I'm freezing,' Anna said. All she wanted was to get inside.

That night she dreamed of the bridge and the parapet, and the boy dancing on it. Threaded into the dream were flashing lights and the wail of an ambulance siren. There was the river smell, dank and reedy, and a gypsy caravan with a fortune-teller on its steps, prophesying doom.

CHAPTER ELEVEN

THE first thing Anna noticed as she crossed the yard to A and E next day was that Daniel's BMW wasn't in its allotted space. Surely he was back. She stood very still, staring at the vacant slot, aware of a feeling like prickling alarm stiffening the back of her neck.

Of course, he could have gone off the precinct to lunch, but that would be unusual on a Monday, the main operating day. Had something happened... happened to *him*? She thought of the ambulances last night. Could he have been involved in an accident along by the river bank? It had been hot last night. He might have gone swimming, gone with James, perhaps... Maybe one of them... She felt sick suddenly, and approached A and E's doors at a run.

The first familiar face she saw was Clive's. He was waiting by the lifts. 'Is Daniel in Theatre?' She tried to sound normal as, with three young medics, they entered the first lift. 'I didn't see his car as I came in, and wondered if he was back.'

'Good Lord, of course, you don't know, do you?'

To her further alarm, she felt Clive grasp her arm as the lift stopped at level three. They got out, Clive still holding her arm, his face grave.

'What are you trying to say?' She snatched herself free. 'Just tell me *what has happened*!'

'There was an accident at Coe Fen late last night. James Mackay and another student went swimming. The friend was daft enough to dive off the bridge par-

162

apet. He struck his head and didn't surface. James got him out, resuscitated him, then collapsed himself. There was a bloke walking his dog on the towpath—he sent for help. The two boys were brought here and, of course, James was recognised in Cas. He's in ITU now with breathing problems. Daniel was here all last night.'

'How is he now...James...this morning?' After the first rush of relief that nothing had happened to Daniel, concern for James came to the fore.

'He arrested twice and they've been shocking him.'

'And the other boy?'

'In the obs ward with slight concussion. He'll probably be discharged today.'

'Oh, God!'

'Exactly!'

'Where's Daniel now?' she asked.

'Getting his head down. He was around until an hour ago, ringing his parents and his sister, who'll be coming down straight away!'

There was a hint of the old insouciance in Clive's manner, and Anna dragged her arm free. 'I'll ring ITU from the office,' she said. Leaving Clive to make his way into Athelstone Ward, she hurried down the corridor.

'Seriously ill.' That was all she got from ITU, which meant, as she very well knew, that James could die. She also knew that she couldn't keep pestering the department with calls. She wanted to go down there, but couldn't do that either, for her own ward routine had to go on as usual—lunches, the quiet hour, the handover report, new patients to be settled in.

During visiting Kate Denver limped into the office, saying that she'd heard about Mr Mackay's brother,

and was it true he was very ill? 'I couldn't help hearing
the nurses talking about it, Sister, and Mr Mackay
hasn't been in today.'

Bad news travels fast, Anna thought, gently telling
the girl that, yes, James Mackay was very ill. 'He res-
cued a friend from drowning last night, Kate, but collapsed afterwards.'

'He must be the hero type, like our Mr Mackay. It
must be in the genes!' She attempted a smile, which
didn't quite come off. 'I hope he gets on for his sake.
Please tell him how upset we all are.'

'Of course,' Anna promised. 'Of course I will.'

But where was Daniel, for heaven's sake? Most
likely back in ITU. Should she ring again? No, she
mustn't. She looked at the telephone. No news was
good news—she tried to hang on to that. Any minute
now Daniel might come up to tell her that James was
improving.

He did come, but not with good news. He came during evening visiting, casually clad in jeans and a thick
sweater, as though he were cold. His hair was scru-
pulously tidy and brushed flat. He had plainly made an
effort, but his eyes were bleak, his face lined and tired.

Anna all but dragged him into the office. 'Thank
goodness you've come! What…is the news?'

He took the chair Kate had vacated earlier on and
sat there with a ramrod-straight back. Anna stood at his
side, wishing they were somewhere private where she
could have given him a hug.

'The news isn't good, Anna. James had a haemor-
rhage, a massive haemoptysis, a couple of hours ago.
With the state his heart is in at present, it's going to
be tricky to transfuse him. The consultant cardiologist
and his registrar are with him now.'

'Oh, no! But James has always been so fit. He'll put up a good fight, I'm sure!'

And maybe I'm talking rubbish, she thought, hearing Daniel go on to say, 'James has had a damaged heart from the age of seven, a legacy of rheumatic fever…'

'Valvular disease?' Her eyes widened.

'Mitral stenosis, yes. It was minor, not progressive, and he had regular checks. To a certain extent he heeded it—when he thought about it, that is—but it didn't stop him doing what he wanted. I think our parents and I had it in mind more than he did. It was one of the reasons I wanted to see him in decent digs—'

'Hence the house,' Anna interrupted quickly.

'Partly, yes. No one knew about his heart, except our parents and myself—and Margot, my ex-wife—during his early teen years.'

Anna nodded, the mention of Daniel's ex-wife giving her a jolt, even amid her worsening fear for James. What a brave but instinctive, *instantaneous* thing he had done, dragging his unconscious friend out of the river, working on him on the bank, so long and relentlessly that he'd collapsed himself. 'I suppose,' she said in a small voice, 'that Kevin Leigh is fighting fit!'

'Not quite. He's concussed, but not seriously so. He may be discharged today. I don't begrudge him his resilience, Anna. I just wish someone a little stronger than James had been around to rescue him.'

His use of her first name, coming just then, made her feel ridiculously weepy. 'Oh, if only there was something I could do to *help*!' she cried out passionately.

'Actually, there is.'

'What? Name it!'

'Is there the remotest chance, do you think, of your

parents being able to accommodate Mother and Dad at
Rivers Lawns? I know it's the height of the season so
the likelihood's pretty remote, but I felt, if you asked
them…'

'I'll do it now—right now while you wait. We *are*
fully booked, but sometimes we get cancellations at the
last moment. I suppose you want one double room and
one single?'

'Ideally, yes.' He got up while she phoned and asked
to be put straight through to her father, explaining what
had happened. There was a wait, the sound of distant
voices, then her reply. 'Oh, *brilliant*, Dad, I'll tell him!'

'They had a cancellation just about lunch. There's a
double room free until Saturday but no single, so your
sister—'

'Oh, I can put her up at the flat. May I?' He held
out his hand for the receiver and spoke to Edward
Chancellor himself. 'It might be after midnight tonight…is that all right?' Anna heard him ask. After a
few more words he put down the phone and huffed out
his breath in relief. 'I can't tell you what a weight that
is off my mind… It's a long drive from Edinburgh and
my parents aren't young.'

'Well, we do like the hotel full, you know!' Anna
attempted to joke a little, then, sobering, asked if there
was anything else she could do, and once again he said
there was…

'It's Rowena.' He was feeling in the pocket of his
jeans, bringing out a scrap of paper. 'This isn't a nice
job, but could you possibly ring her and tell her that
James is seriously ill? She has a right to know.'

'Yes, yes…of *course*!'

'This is her Singapore number.' The scrap of paper
exchanged hands. 'I tried myself at midday, which

would be evening time for them, so she was probably out. I could get no reply. I think if you rang about ten when you got home tonight you'd catch her before she'd be getting up.'

Anna nodded, thinking, Poor Rowena, what a shock for her. She had been so reluctant to leave James. Could that fortune-teller at the fair have foreseen this? She shivered involuntarily.

Rowena's reaction to her call across the world some four hours later was to say that she was coming home on the first available flight. She was horrified, yet calm and decisive, leading Anna to think that, despite her appearance and dotty air, Rowena Delter was a force to be reckoned with.

Throughout the night Anna slept in snatches, even her dreams asking questions... Would James survive until the morning? Was the Mackay family with him? How soon would Rowena arrive? Would Daniel manage to work?

Her mother woke her at six with a cup of tea. 'They're here, darling.' She meant the Mackays. 'They booked in just after one, Daddy was still up. He said Daniel and his sister saw them in, then went back to the hospital.'

'Is James still alive?'

'He was then. Aren't you going to phone?'

Anna was already lifting the receiver on her bedside table. She dialled the hospital, getting through to ITU and receiving the guarded reply that James had had a comfortable night.

'Unless you're a relative you get no sensible info,' she said, gulping down her tea and going through to shower. But at least he was alive...he was alive...he was alive! He'd survived two nights. That had to be hopeful…*had* to be! Now all she wanted was to get to the hospital, see Daniel and find out the score.

She ran straight into him as she crossed the car park a little over an hour later. He and a tall dark girl, who looked remarkably like him, were standing beside a red Volvo, the girl pushing back wayward hair. 'My sister, Ella,' said Daniel, introducing her. 'Ella, this is Anna…Anna Chancellor.'

'Daniel's told me how helpful you've been.' Ella Sterne had a good look at Anna, but her smile was warm, as was the grip of her hand.

'How's James? How is he this morning?' Anna asked in a rush. 'I rang ITU before I got up, but got no real news other than that he'd got through the night. How is he now?'

Brother and sister expelled long breaths. 'Well,' Daniel said, a smile stretching his face, which was grey with fatigue, 'he's tolerated the blood transfusion with only a slight rise in temperature and no dramatic worsening of his heart.'

'Does he know you?'

'Oh, yes.' It was Ella who answered. 'But we can only go in for a couple of minutes. He's all wired-up and everything, like a bionic man! Your father was brilliant at the hotel last night, welcoming Mother and Dad in. It's such a relief to us, isn't it, Dan, to have them nearby and in a nice place? Thanks for your part in it all.'

'I did very little.' Anna looked at Daniel.

Ella was getting into her car, bound for Maitland House and some sleep. 'That's what you should be doing, too,' she said to her brother before she moved off.

Anna told Daniel about Rowena as they went into

the hospital. 'Seems there's a good deal to the fairy-doll girl that doesn't show on the surface,' he said, echoing Anna's thought of the night before. 'Of course...' His hand came under her elbow as they went up the ramp. 'It could be love.' His hand tightened on the soft, bare skin of her arm. 'And love is a very potent force—its powers know no bounds.'

'That's a very profound remark from a man who's been up most of the night,' she teased gently, but, glancing up at him, surprised a wistful expression in his eyes and found herself shaken by a fierce and almost primeval longing to tell him how much she loved him. But it was scarcely the time, and certainly not the place, so all she said when they parted at the lifts was, 'Don't work too hard today.'

During the ward round, shortly after eleven, he was his usual professional self. Through in Occupational Therapy he watched Kate Denver working a treadle to increase her range of movement and strengthen her lower limbs. He watched her go up steps and come back down them, learned that she was able to flex her knee to ninety degrees, then gave her the news she'd been hoping and waiting for—that he could sign her off.

'In other words, you can go home, Kate, as from tomorrow a.m. However...' He raised a brow. 'Please, don't go riding that motorbike just yet, and remember we want to see you back here in four weeks' time to have your brace removed.'

'*Would* I forget?' Kate was wondering how James was, but didn't like to enquire.

'And even after that,' Daniel persisted, 'you'll need loads more physio to get your leg into proper shape.'

'I'll do anything and everything I have to,' she promised, 'and thank you for all you've done!'

The midday edition of the *Seftonbridge Echo* carried a report on the river rescue at the foot of its front page. Pam Fiske, her face serious, showed it to Anna over lunch. WILL THEY NEVER LEARN? it was headed.

Nineteen-year-old James Mackay, a first-year student at Corpus Christi College, is fighting for his life today in Seftonbridge General Hospital, after saving his friend, Kevin Leigh, from drowning on Sunday night. The two had gone swimming after dark, and were diving from Coe Fen Bridge, when Leigh failed to surface. Mackay dragged him out, performed life-saving measures and collapsed himself with breathing difficulties. Leigh, who suffered slight concussion, was too upset to comment. Once again the river authorities and police are stressing the danger of diving from bridges, especially after dark.

'Heavens!' Anna was transfixed. 'I must show it to Daniel!'

'I should imagine he's seen it by now. Tell me,' Pam asked, spooning up the last of her raspberry ripple, 'what are his parents like?'

'I haven't met them yet, but the sister is like Daniel—tall, dark, forceful and striking. I wouldn't like to fall out with her! She was just going off to get some sleep when I arrived this morning.'

'James is the baby of the family, isn't he? Must have come late in life, which could be, just *could* be, why he's not too robust.'

'Maybe,' Anna said carefully, keeping quiet about James's cardiac defect, remembering that no one but his family and Daniel's ex-wife knew about it. It was odd, she thought as she went back to the ward, how Margot Mackay kept slipping into her mind more since James's brush with death.

Getting back to the hotel that evening shortly after five, she saw Daniel in the lounge with an elderly couple, who were obviously his parents. The tall Ella was pouring tea and facing her way, but it was Daniel who caught sight of her as she crossed the lobby on the way to the family flat. He got up and beckoned, so in she went, wishing she'd had time to freshen up and get out of her uniform.

As she was introduced, she could see the resemblance between Mrs Mackay and her daughter. Mr Mackay senior, she thought, resembled James, with his wide smile, fresh complexion and hair that had once been red. She was asked to have tea with them, which she did, set at ease and encouraged by Daniel's wink which allied her to him.

'We so appreciate being able to stay here,' Mrs Mackay said, 'although, naturally, we wish it were in happier circumstances. Still...' She smiled. 'The news was good when we left the hospital just now. You explain, Daniel—these medical terms tie me up!'

'The good news is—' Daniel's eyes rested on Anna's hot face '—that James's heart has now settled into normal sinus rhythm. He's on digoxin at present, but they hope to reduce the dosage tomorrow, if he keeps on as he's doing.'

'That's *fantastic*!' Anna said, smiling round at them all.

'He was a different lad this afternoon,' Mr Mackay put in. 'When we saw him last night I didn't know what to think—well, to be frank, I thought the worst.

Of course, it's early days yet, but I have a good feeling about him now, which I didn't have last night.'

'We're going back there this evening,' Ella said, 'although we'll probably spend most of the time in the waiting-room because they literally trickle us in but we've got that feeling of wanting to be near... You know how it is.'

'Yes, I do,' Anna assured her. 'Families should be together at a time like this.'

They chatted for a little while after that, the newspaper report being mentioned.

Mr Mackay—a retired chiropractor—told Anna that after his working life in London was finished, he couldn't wait to get back to his native Scotland. 'Great place to live,' he said.

Ella asked Anna about her work, while she, in turn, asked about Ella's children, although never forgetting, not for a single second, the long, rangy figure of Daniel who was sitting there, eating a scone.

It was Mr Mackay who, when she got up to go, suggested that she have dinner with them one evening. 'You see, if James keeps making progress, we may not always visit in the late evening—just have a good afternoon session with him and let other people have a look in.'

'Yes, do join us. Can you manage Thursday?' Mrs Mackay raised questioning brows, so like Daniel's that Anna was quite unnerved.

'Thursday would be fine.'

'Am I invited?' That was Daniel, looking amused.

'I expect we'll have to put up with you.' His sister grinned. 'But we'll have to eat early, Dad.' She looked across at her father. 'That's the night, if all goes well, that I'll be travelling back to Cornwall. By then the kids will just about have driven Garth round the bend!'

Everyone laughed, including Daniel, who escorted Anna to the foot of the stairs.

'That was a very pleasant interlude,' he said. 'You've got Dad eating out of your hand, exactly the same as me!'

'That will be the day!' she replied, laughing and running upstairs.

CHAPTER TWELVE

AT NOON next day James was proclaimed well enough to leave ITU and be transferred to the cardiac ward. This Anna heard from Daniel who, although he was operating all day, found time to slip up to the ward at lunchtime to tell her the good news.

'Why not nip down and see him?' he suggested. 'He's ready for visitors now.'

'I'll go during my lunch-break so as not to clash with the afternoon people,' she said.

'Do that.' They exchanged happy glances, he standing there tall and thin in his theatre blues and hair-concealing cap.

'It's wonderful news!' she said breathlessly.

'I know...the absolute best!' And he bent and kissed her, careless of where they stood, or where they were, or who might see them. The anxious time was over.

As it happened, Anna did clash with someone when she went down to the cardiac ward. She met Rowena, who had come straight from the airport. She was sitting as close to James as she dared, hanging onto his hand.

'Good for you, Rowena.' Anna was looking at James, who was lying propped up, still attached to a monitor which was making all the right noises and squiggles. An oxygen mask lay nearby. He looked a little flushed over his cheek-bones, but otherwise much the same. 'You gave us a fright, James.'

'I gave myself one.' He smiled tiredly. 'Still, I'll soon be out of here now.'

Staying just seconds, for James was only allowed one visitor at a time, Anna made her way out. How Rowena had got in at this timé she couldn't begin to guess—most likely by saying that she was his partner and had just flown in from Singapore.

Out in the waiting-room was a youth of roughly James's age. He was in street clothes, but the dressing on his head alerted Anna at once. Kevin Leigh, if I'm not mistaken, she thought, passing by with a smile.

During the afternoon she heard from one of the cardiac staff that James Mackay's girlfriend had very nearly given Kevin a black eye to go with his concussed head. 'I've never heard anything like it, Sister Chancellor. She really tore him off a strip!'

Still, as I've said before, Anna thought, laughing in spite of herself, Rowena is a force to be reckoned with. Poor Kevin. He was probably feeling guilty enough already, without being harangued.

On Thursday morning Daniel and Clive came to see the newly post-op patients and to do a full round. Anna was just tidying up after it, the two surgeons having gone off, when her phone rang for about the tenth time. On picking up the receiver, a woman's voice, sounding slightly impatient, said in her ear, 'I'd like to speak to Mr Mackay. Your switchboard said he'd be on the ward.'

'Who's speaking, please?' Damn the switchboard, Anna thought. They know better than to—

'I'm Dr Mackay...Dr Margot Mackay, and this is a London call, so if you could hurry...'

Anna's mouth went dry, while her heart gave a violent leap. 'Mr Mackay has just left the ward, but he may be in our neighbouring one. If you'll hold on, I'll enquire for you.' It was his wife, wasn't it? His ex-wife, ringing from London! Somehow…somehow she pressed the right button for Athelstone Ward and heard Pam's brisk voice. 'Sister Fiske speaking.'

'Pam…' Now her throat was closing up. 'Pam, I've got a personal caller on my line for Mr Mackay. Is he still in the ward?'

'In the corridor. I'll get him—put the caller through!'

Anna did so only too willingly. Replacing the receiver, she sat down, staring at the cream and black instrument, her heart still thundering. Daniel's wife. So they were still in touch, and she was in London, not abroad. Perhaps she was ringing to ask about James, whom she'd known as a boy.

On the other hand, how would she have known about him unless Daniel had told her? He must have known she was in London, and where to find her. Perhaps when he was in Town last week they had spent time together. She might even have been the 'friend' he had stayed with in the Barbican.

Over lunch Pam mentioned the call before Anna even asked. 'She was obviously a member of the family,' she said. 'Probably a cousin. Anyway, she was ringing from St Mildred's. She mentioned that before I handed her over. She sounded impatient, a bit hoity-toity…'

'Yes, I noticed that myself.'

'Anyway, they were talking together some minutes.'

'I expect,' Anna said, forbearing to tell Pam who the caller had been, because she'd have gone on and on about it non-stop, 'she was ringing to ask about James.'

'Well, I went out, of course, and left them to it, so

I don't really know,' Pam informed her, looking a little smug.

Anna's thoughts—and she was only picking at her lunch—continued to escalate. Perhaps they would get together again—divorced couples sometimes did. Perhaps she and Daniel and James would all live together in the Elvington Road house. And that was the worst thought of all.

She would have given a great deal to have got out of tonight's dinner with the Mackays. Still, I can't, and that's that, she told herself at six o'clock that evening, standing under the pelting shower. She was trying to whip up anger, and direct it straight at Daniel for being the way he had with her over the past three months, but fairness made her admit that he had never pressured her and had never set out to seduce her when she had bucked at an affair. And thank goodness I didn't go to bed with him, she thought. If I had—with *her* on the scene again—it would have been the Rob-and-me scenario, all over again.

Emerging from the shower, not feeling much better, she nevertheless made a concentrated effort to look her absolute best. She slid her dresses along the rail in the wardrobe, passing over the one she thought of as '*that* dress'—the one with the mended neck. She was tempted to wear it—serve Daniel right—but he might not even notice. In the end she decided on a silken tunic in a soft shade of aquamarine, with palazzo pants to match. She dressed her hair in a single plait which she drew over one shoulder, clipped on gold earrings, sprayed on perfume and made her way downstairs.

They were there, in a group, the handsome Mackays, Daniel and his father springing up at her approach. Daniel pulled out a chair and Ella said in her down-to-earth fashion, 'Good, you're on time.' As she didn't want to be late starting off on her long drive to Cornwall, they went straight into the dining-room, Daniel sitting next to Anna, Ella on her right, the older Mackays facing them. Mr Mackay seemed incapable of taking his eyes off their guest till their prawn cocktail starter arrived and they all began to eat.

Naturally enough the main topic of conversation was James's continuing recovery. He had been up for a little while that afternoon, and was already becoming irked by what he called being 'ordered about'.

'He'll need a fortnight's professionally supervised convalescence, then the rest of his vacation period with us in Scotland,' Mrs Mackay said.

'I think you'll have to accommodate Rowena as well.' Daniel stirred at Anna's side. 'When I went in to see James at teatime he told me that he and she were moving into her bedsit together in Grafton Road. He said he was sorry about the Elvington Road house, but neither of them wanted to live there.'

His parents looked startled. Anna stared at Daniel, dismay for him plain on her face, but Ella laughed. 'Yes, well, that's younger brothers for you—ingratitude and all that!'

Mr and Mrs Mackay still hadn't spoken when Daniel went on to say, 'I've felt all along that he wasn't too keen. There was no enthusiasm, no jumping up and down.'

'Good job you've not signed anything yet.' Jock Mackay spluttered a little, dabbing his napkin against his mouth.

'I intend to sign the contract tomorrow, Dad. I'm not backing out,' Daniel said firmly. 'I want the house, I did from the start. It has great Victorian charm.'

There was a brief silence which Anna broke. 'I know what Daniel means,' she said. 'I enjoyed living there, even in just the top part. I hated moving out. It's an unusual house with a lovely atmosphere. I think it must always have been lived in by happy people.'

Meeting Anna's eyes and blinking her own, Mrs Mackay made the point that they ought to meet Rowena. 'She must,' she said fairly, 'think a lot of him to fly halfway across the world to be with him when he was ill. Perhaps we're apt to forget...' she looked sideways at her husband '...that James is adult. He knows what he wants and perhaps being ill has made this even more clear to him.'

'Well said, Mother!' Daniel applauded. He didn't, Anna noticed, look at all put out by James's defection. Perhaps if he and the cool-sounding Margot were going to get together, having the whole house all to themselves would be the best thing of all.

'No end of people have enquired about him,' Daniel continued. 'Guess who rang to get news of him today?'

'Prince Charles?' Mr Mackay suggested, while Anna stiffened because she knew what was coming...

'Margot!' Daniel supplied. 'She's doing a locum in St Mildred's A and E, before going abroad again. We've still got mutual friends at Milly's, and one of them had Tuesday's copy of the *Seftonbridge Echo*, and showed Margot the bit about James. So she rang me, which was good of her, I thought. I told her he was doing just fine.'

'Bit of shock for you, wasn't it, her turning up?' Mr Mackay said dourly.

'A surprise, not a shock. I thought she was still in darkest Africa! James, I might say, was very laid back when I gave him her message.'

'Good for him,' Ella said, sounding amazingly like her father. Then she changed the subject by asking Anna about her painting. 'Dan told me you were artistic, and had loads of talent.'

'That was nice of him!' Slowly but surely Anna was beginning to hope again.

'So, when do you have time to do it?'

'During off-duty weekends and long evenings in the summer.'

'And do you go out in a smock with an easel and palette, and sit on the river bank, looking all arty and interesting?'

'No, I do not!' Anna laughed, 'I'd feel too self-conscious. I go off with a block and a set of pencils, and hope no one will notice me!'

'I think you would be noticed, Anna, dear, in the dimmest, darkest dungeon!' Emboldened by two glasses of Chablis, and having ordered a brandy with his cheese, Mr Mackay beamed across at her, his blue eyes moistening.

'You never spoke a truer word, Dad!' In full view of everyone Daniel put his hand over Anna's as it lay on the tablecloth.

After dinner when the older Mackays were taking a stroll in the grounds, Daniel went off to get Ella's car filled up with petrol and oil. Ella and Anna, finding a quiet spot in the lounge, sat down to talk again, Anna asking how old Ella's children were.

'Eight, six and four,' she said, bringing a folder of photographs out of her bag. 'Have a look through them. They'll all of the kids, taken fairly recently.'

Anna pored over them, while Ella explained which child was which. There were children in a sandpit, children up a tree, children sliding down chutes—but the last snapshot was different. It showed a much younger Ella, Daniel and James standing against a background of heathland and trees. Standing a little to the side was a woman in shorts, holding a cricket bat.

'Is that Daniel's wife?' Anna's hand trembled slightly as she held out the snap. Ella took it from her. 'Yes, that's Margot. I'd forgotten that one was there.'

'What was she like?' Anna couldn't help the question.

'Attractive, amusing, devious and selfish to the bone. Wanted everything in her own ditch, which is death to any relationship. Why they didn't just settle for an affair, I'll never know. It was Dan really. He was keen to get married, have a family and settle down. He wanted everything far too soon, and he thought she was the one. Decent men of twenty-six aren't all that clued up, you know. Now, of course, he's gone all cautious, won't commit himself at all. Anyway, here he comes, we'd better stop gossiping.' Taking the photographs from Anna, Ella snapped them shut in her bag.

Watching Daniel approaching them, his light grey jacket open for coolness, his hair black under the lights, a resolute set to his jaw, Anna felt a swoop of longing for him so intense she could hardly stand up.

'Your carriage awaits,' he said to Ella, but smiling at them both. 'The parents are in the drive, waiting to see you off.'

It was nine o'clock, not quite dark, but the lights had been switched on in the grounds and drive, giving Ella's face a pallid look as she said her goodbyes. Once she had gone, Mr and Mrs Mackay, wearied after the strain of the past few days, retired to their room, expressing the hope that they'd see Anna next day. That left only Anna and Daniel standing at the side of the drive, watching a taxi bringing new guests to the hotel.

'I haven't got my car—I came here in Ella's. What do you say to grabbing that cab when it comes back empty?' Daniel was watching it unload. 'Then we can go to my flat for a nightcap, round the evening off.'

'Daniel...'

'No arguments!'

'I wasn't going to argue. I need to get my bag.'

'Get it, then, and I'll nab the taxi.'

Off she went like a dart. It had happened, he had asked her. This was her chance to proposition him, her chance to talk things out, to tell him he didn't need to make promises or pledges of any kind, for she now wanted what he did—to settle for an affair.

In the taxi they held hands, but didn't sit especially close and, aware of the driver in front, talked only of casual things, Daniel asking her how she was getting on, living at home.

'All right so far, but, then, of course, I've only been there a week and a bit,' she pointed out, watching the traffic lights flick to red.

'This week seems to have lasted for ever.'

'Bad times always drag. It's the happy ones that race by.' They were moving on again, turning left for Magdalene Bridge and the start of Grange Road.

'Will you take Ellison's flat, do you think?' He was feeling in his pocket for change.

'It's his mother's flat, and, no, I've decided against it. I mean,' she added as they began to draw up outside Maitland House, 'it would look pretty rude to my parents to leave again quite so soon.'

Standing out on the pavement while he paid off the taxi, she began to feel decidedly twitchy. Perhaps she shouldn't have come. His flat was on the ground floor so it took no time at all to get inside—into the small entrance hall that smelled of new carpet and paint. He ushered her through to the sitting-room, switching on a lamp. As he drew the curtains over the window, Anna was very nervous. Instead, she kept talking, she had to keep talking. 'What a lovely room!' she exclaimed.

'It's a very nice flat, but I'm still looking forward to moving into Elvington Road.' He motioned her to sit, and she took one of the chairs.

'James won't be with you, though.' She wondered why he was still standing up.

'No, that's very true but, as the saying goes, I'm not my brother's keeper, and if James's future lies with Rowena, so be it.' He smiled. 'I've always realised, anyway, that in two years' time, once he's graduated, he'll probably want to leave Seftonbridge. James is a volatile lad!'

'Yes, I suppose.' Anna looked at the carpet, seeing his feet start to move. Perhaps now she could start... Perhaps now she could say...

'What would you like to drink?' The feet passed her as he started to make his way to a cocktail cabinet on the other side of the room.

'I don't want a drink.' Her voice shook and he turned. The next second she was in his arms, crushed so tight and hard against him that her breath was expelled in a grunt, so tight that she could feel every male inch of him imprinting itself on her in exactly the right places. She held him with little sighs and moans, her hands gripped round his back.

'My Anna...my Anna... Oh, Anna, my love!' He carried her into the bedroom. Clothes came off in swift glides and tugs. Within seconds they lay, turned towards one another on the double bed, the streetlamp through the thin blind filtering light on their naked forms.

They made love quickly—neither could wait. Urgency lent them wings, but it was passion that sent them soaring and skimming over the mountaintops, dipping and rising in perfect unison to the goal they knew they would both reach.

In the peaceful sweetness of the aftermath he told her how wonderful she was. 'But I always knew you would be.'

'No surprise, then?' She turned her head, meeting his eyes an inch from hers.

'Don't tease, you witch. I love you, and loving is a serious business.'

'I *am* serious, never more so, and I love you, too.'

'Enough to move in with me…here in the flat, then later to Elvington Road?'

'Enough,' she said, 'for anything.' Oh, was she really hearing this. 'Do you think,' she said, 'you could kiss me again? I just simply never thought—'

But she couldn't speak any more. He was kissing her thoroughly, every inch of her. When he'd finished, and it took a long time, he made himself even more clear.

'I'm talking marriage here… I hope you are… Of course you may still be holding a torch for Dudley.'

'Not any more, not any more, and of course I'll marry you, but you always said—'

'I know what I said, but James, nearly losing his life, has made me see mine in a rather different perspective, so, to a lesser extent did talking to my ex on the phone. Listening to her going on about her brand-new freedom—she wasn't talking about James the whole time, you know—made me realise what a fool I was to have allowed a failed marriage to blight my existence. And I'll tell you something else, my darling.' He moved her golden plait—which had somehow survived his previous onslaught—under her chin like a rope. 'I fell in love with you during my first week at the General—with the pretty little Sister, so soon to wed Robert-the-Dud!'

'Now you *are* pulling my leg!'

'I'm not. Why do you think I went on leave the week you had your send-off party? I couldn't face it, that's why, so I made myself scarce. When I came back and you weren't married, I began to hope—'

'That I'd have an affair with you?'

'For my sins, yes, at that time, yes. Am I forgiven?' He moved over her again. She could see him above her, the love in his eyes, the intent on his face. Her body arched, her arms went up to latch about his neck, and she just had time to nod her head before they made love again.

The two sets of parents were delighted, if surprised. 'Best news I've had in years!' Edward Chancellor said. Mr Mackay went on and on about Daniel being a lucky chap. Mrs Mackay folded Anna into a perfumed embrace and kissed her on both cheeks. Lois Chancellor hugged her daughter and whispered, 'Love you.' She kissed her prospective son-in-law and kept her fingers crossed.

She needn't have worried. On a golden day in mid-September Anna and Daniel were married at the Shire Hall Register Office up on Castle Hill. James was best man, and Julie—over from Ireland—was bridesmaid with Rowena, who was looking just as much a fairy doll as ever with a diamond stud in her nose.

And life was to be good to Daniel and Anna. During the following ten years they had three children—two boys and a girl—which satisfactorily filled all the bedrooms at the Elvington Road house. Daniel passed his consultancy exams and took over from Sir Guy. Anna still nursed, but through an agency only, which meant she could choose her hours. Never had she thought she could be so happy.

'Which only goes to show,' Daniel said, when she told him, 'that love makes the world go round!'

MILLS & BOON®

Makes
any time
special

Enjoy a romantic novel from
Mills & Boon®

Presents...   *Enchanted*™   TEMPTATION.

Historical Romance™   ⫟**MEDICAL
ROMANCE**™

MAT1

FREE
4 BOOKS
AND A SURPRISE GIFT!

We would like to take this opportunity to thank you for reading this Mills & Boon® book by offering you the chance to take FOUR more specially selected titles from the Medical Romance™ series absolutely FREE! We're also making this offer to introduce you to the benefits of the Reader Service™ —

★ FREE home delivery
★ FREE monthly Newsletter
★ FREE gifts and competitions
★ Exclusive Reader Service discounts
★ Books available before they're in the shops

Accepting these FREE books and gift places you under no obligation to buy; you may cancel at any time, even after receiving your free shipment. Simply complete your details below and return the entire page to the address below. *You don't even need a stamp!*

YES! Please send me 4 free Medical Romance books and a surprise gift. I understand that unless you hear from me, I will receive 6 superb new titles every month for just £2.40 each, postage and packing free. I am under no obligation to purchase any books and may cancel my subscription at any time. The free books and gift will be mine to keep in any case.

MOEC

Ms/Mrs/Miss/Mr ....Initials ....
BLOCK CAPITALS PLEASE

Surname ....

Address ....

....

....Postcode ....

Send this whole page to:
UK: FREEPOST CN81, Croydon, CR9 3WZ
EIRE: PO Box 4546, Kilcock, County Kildare (stamp required)

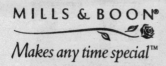

Marriages by Arrangement

A MARRIAGE HAS BEEN ARRANGED
by Anne Weale

Pierce Sutherland is the only man Holly has ever wanted, but her glamorous blonde stepsister is more his type. So when Pierce proposes a marriage of convenience, can Holly's pride allow her to accept?

TO TAME A PROUD HEART
by Cathy Williams

Francesca Wade is determined to prove her worth to her employer. Yet one night of passion has her out of Oliver Kemp's office and up the aisle—with a man too proud to love her, but too honourable to leave her!

NEVER A BRIDE by Diana Hamilton

Jake Winter was every woman's fantasy—and Claire's husband! But their marriage was a purely business arrangement—so how was Claire to tell Jake she'd fallen in love with him?

**Look out for *Marriages* by Arrangement
in July 2000**